EMOTIONALLY UNAVAILABLE

1

CONTACT ME

IG: @keishaervin

Twitter: @keishaervin

Facebook: www.facebook.com/keisha.ervin

Pinterest: Keisha Ervin

ervinkeisha@yahoo.com

YouTube: Color Me Pynk Channel

2

To My Readers,

After writing Chyna Black, I had no intentions on ever writing a sequel. I'd gone through the fire. I'd made it. I thought I'd found myself. I thought I was perfect but I was young. Little did I know, more trouble was ahead. I was 26-years-old and I had it all, except a man. I prayed day and night for God to send me someone and he did. I wasn't specific though in what I wanted, so God sent me exactly what I asked for - a man.

For five and a half years, I went through an emotional hell. During that time, you all, my readers, asked for a Chyna Black 2. I told myself, "hell no! I don't want these people to know my business". I was preaching to you all to love yourself and know your worth through my books and social media posts and I, myself, was living a lie. I was just as broken and confused as you all were. I was embarrassed of myself. I hadn't found myself at all. I was still going through the motions and learning new things day by day.

I released Chyna Black in 2005; it's 2015 now. Ten years have passed by since I wrote about the young, naïve, insecure, passionate, hot-headed girl named Chyna Black. When I began to write Emotionally Unavailable, my original plan was to write something totally different. I found myself unable to get my vision across or my words on paper because something was missing. It wasn't meant for me to tell the story of pain and discovery through the eyes of an imaginary character. It was meant for me to tell my story.

Going through the turmoil I went through not only taught me how to be a better me but it taught me how to be a better mother, friend and overall person. I told myself that there was no need to feel ashamed. My testimony will be a blessing for somebody out there that is still going through a toxic relationship.

I no longer care if I'm viewed as dumb. I didn't have it all together then and I still don't now. Have I come a long way? Yes. I thank God everyday for the lessons I have learned. I'm stronger, wiser, happier and at peace. The stories I tell in this book took place from the ages of 26-29. I pray that my testimony gives you a better perception of me and helps heal some scars a man has etched on your heart.

Keisha

P.S. - I want to give special thanks to Nikita Moore. Thank you for being there to answer all of the research questions I had about book one. You were a godsend.☺

"I USED TO LIKE THE IDEA OF PEOPLE THINKING THAT I HAD IT ALL TOGETHER. NOW I CAN'T WAIT TO TELL THEM HOW MUCH OF A MESS I WAS AND SHOW THEM WHAT THE POWER OF GOD CAN DO." – SOURCE UNKNOWN

THIS WAS ME THEN...

CHAPTER 1

She was the baddest. He was the realest. They were the illest couple alive. Chyna Danae Black was on cloud 9. It was only a minute before the clock struck midnight. The year 2013 was fast approaching. That New Year's Eve she had everything a woman her age could ever want. At the age of 31, she had a beautiful daughter, a thriving career as a national best-selling author, a beautiful home and a man she loved more than life itself.

She and Tyreik had been together on and off since she was 16. He was the love of her life. From the moment she laid eyes on him she couldn't see past him. He was her moon, her stars and everything up above. They'd had their fair share of ups and downs. He wasn't perfect and neither was she.

In the beginning of their relationship, she and Tyreik put each other through it. He cheated; she cheated, got pregnant with his baby and had an abortion. After the abortion, Tyreik couldn't bear to look at her, so he left her for the same chick he'd cheated on her with. The broad's name was Rema.

After breaking up, Chyna nearly had a nervous breakdown. She began to spiral out of control. She started messing wit' her high school crush, LP, got pregnant by him and had her daughter. It wasn't until she had India that she began to pull her life together. She wrote her first book and became a household name. Tyreik realized what a mistake he'd made by letting her go and came begging for forgiveness. After a lot of persuasion, Chyna finally let down her guard and gave him another chance.

Since then, they'd broken up numerous times, only to get back together. No matter how much they tried to stay away from one another, they were like magnets to each other. The struggle for dominance, distrust, disrespect and infidelity always played a huge factor in their discord. But that night everything was good. Chyna and Tyriek couldn't keep their hands off one another. They were both drunk and in love.

In Tyreik's eyes, Chyna was the baddest bitch he'd ever seen. He would never consider wifin' another chick. Homegirl stayed stuntin' on hoes. She never left the house looking a hot mess. Her style game was always on point. She turned heads whenever she entered a room.

Chyna had a face you couldn't take your eyes off of. She was breathtakingly beautiful. Her round, doe-shaped eyes were accentuated with black, gel liner and demi, wispie lashes. Her chiseled cheekbones were contoured to the gawds. When she grinned, her deep dimples exposed the childlike innocence she tried so hard to conceal. Her sumptuous, full lips were painted red.

Chyna's smooth, caramel skin glistened underneath the strobe lights. Going for a minimalist yet chic look, she wore her jet black hair parted down the middle and pulled back into a low, sleek ponytail.

Mama looked cool and sophisticated in a sleeveless, flesh tone top that showcased the fact that she wore no bra. The curves of her hips and bountiful ass filled out every inch of the matching midi skirt she rocked. A pair of nude, gladiator, Givenchy, pointed toe heels completed her ensemble. Chyna resembled a bronzed goddess. You couldn't tell her she wasn't the shit.

Her man was no slouch either. Tyreik was always mistaken for the rapper 50 Cent. The two men looked like identical twins. Tyreik was as dark as night. He possessed menacing, dark brown eyes, a trimmed beard, succulent lips and straight, white teeth. He stood at 6 feet tall and weighed 185 pounds. His chest, biceps and stomach were all chiseled and perfectly crafted by God. The nigga was buff as fuck.

Tyreik's eyes and lips were what captured Chyna's heart the most. He had an undeniable sex appeal that she couldn't resist. He had several, different, huge tattoos but the ones that stood out the most was the one on his chest that read *Death before Dishonor* and the mural of Chyna's face on his right forearm.

He stayed laced in the flyest clothes, rocked the most expensive jewels and drove a bad-ass ride. It'd been years since he sold his last brick. Selling dope had become too big of a risk. Tyreik got tired of constantly looking over his shoulder and being under police surveillance. It didn't help that Chyna stayed down his throat about getting out of the game either.

It took a while for the money he had saved to dry up. Now at the age of 37, he was left wondering what he was going to do with his life. He was damn near 40 and had no career ambition. He was basically coasting along. If it wasn't for Chyna, he'd be destitute. She kept him afloat.

Tyreik hated asking for handouts but working a 9 to 5 just wasn't him. All he knew how to do was sell crack. Chyna didn't mind holding her man down until he figured out what he wanted to do with his life. He'd taken care of her for years. Eventually, Tyreik would pull it together and get back on his feet.

No one knew that he was financially challenged. From the outside looking in, he looked like a million bucks. Chicks stayed on his dick, not knowing that his pockets were flat. The little income he had coming in came from promoting parties with his homeboy Kingston. The New Year's Eve party they were at was being thrown by Kingston and Tyreik. Despite his financial woes, Chyna's biggest problem was dealing with Tyreik's groupies.

He and Chyna stayed arguing over a bitch. Hoes were always trying to get at him. It didn't look good when he was in club pics with random, scantily clad women.

Chicks stayed under his Instagram page leaving inappropriate comments and being extra. They even direct messaged him nude pics and pussy shots. Whenever he stayed out late, Chyna feared he was cheating on her. It had been two years since their last incident but Chyna hadn't gotten over the betrayal.

Don't get it twisted though; Chyna wasn't some basic bitch that couldn't pull another man. Dudes constantly tried to step to her but she shut that shit down out of respect for her man. Despite their constant bickering, her heart belonged to Tyreik. She couldn't see herself with anyone else.

With all of their friends around them, she stood safe in his arms. Chyna looked deep inside his eyes and thanked God for him. After over ten years of being together, they were heading into another as one. Tyreik gazed back at Chyna. She was his baby. He'd wifed her at a young age and years later she was still his #1 rider. Babygirl was the truth. Not a lot of people had been loyal to him over the years but Chyna held him down no matter what.

He'd fucked up quite a few times throughout their relationship but at the core of him Chyna was his reason for living. She made him want to be a better man, even though he didn't always live up to the expectations of what a good man was supposed to be. He knew it was time for him to kick his old habits and settle all the way down. He just needed a little more time. Living a fast life was all he knew. The streets were constantly calling him. He couldn't sit down and wasn't ready to be a family man just yet. But as he stared deep into Chyna's brown eyes, he vowed to do his best to give her the world.

"I love you, big head." He confessed holding her securely in his big, muscular arms.

"I love you too." Chyna smiled as the partygoers in the club counted down to one.

"HAPPY NEW YEAR!" She and Tyreik shouted.

Chyna jumped up and down with glee as a cloud of confetti fell from the ceiling. Happiness filled her heart. Tyreik leaned down and placed his lips upon hers. Chyna's lips still tasted just as sweet as they did the first time he kissed her. Chyna instantly became entranced by the taste of his tongue on hers. She could stay in his arms just like that forever.

"Get a room!" Chyna's best friend, Brooke, yelled breaking up their make out session.

Chyna came up for air and laughed.

"Let me find out you a hater."

"Never, boo boo, but Happy New Year, friend!" Brooke stretched her long arms out for a hug.

Chyna released her arms from around Tyreik and reached up to hug her friend. Her petite, 5'3 frame was swallowed up by Brooke's tall, statuesque physique. Brooke was drop-dead gorgeous. She stood tall at 5'11 and possessed the creamiest cocoa brown skin Chyna had ever seen.

Brooke could've easily been Naomi Campbell's younger sister. The only difference between the two women was that Brooke wore her hair short and low. The low cut framed her face perfectly. Along with Brooke, her other best friend, Asia, Asia's husband and Chyna's friend, Jaylen, Tyreik's pot'nahs Kingston and Juelz, along with their chicks, took over the V.I.P section at the Coliseum.

Unlike Chyna and Brooke, Asia wasn't a party girl. She and Jaylen were happily married with a beautiful son named Aiden. Asia spent her time being a loving wife and mother. Her days of staying in the streets were over. Even though she wasn't into the street life anymore, Asia was still one of the prettiest women to ever walk the face of the earth.

She was a mixture of Asian and African decent, giving her an exotic look. Her husband Jaylen was a NBA star that played for the Miami Heat. His career was winding down but Jaylen was still one of the best in the league. Asia and Jaylen split their time between Miami and St. Louis. Chyna barely got to see them but they still were two of her closest confidants.

"You cute tonight." Brooke gave her a once over glance.

"You know I stay on fleek." Chyna swung her ponytail to the side. "Ain't that what the kids say?"

"Girl, don't ask me," Brooke said with a laugh.

"How you doing, Brooke?" Tyreik spoke loudly.

They'd been around each other for over an hour and she hadn't bothered to acknowledge his presence.

"I'm good." Brooke replied not bothering to give him eye contact.

She couldn't stand Tyreik. If it wasn't for Chyna, she wouldn't have even been in the same room as him.

"You got a light?" Kingston asked Tyreik as he pulled out a few Cuban cigars.

Chyna didn't really care for Kingston. He was a popular club promoter that brought in the biggest names in music, movies and TV to host parties. He was also one of the biggest hoes in St. Louis. He stayed with a different chick and had several kids by several different women.

Chyna didn't even bother learning the chicks' names anymore. Kingston was constantly asking Tyreik to hit the club with him even when they weren't working. Chyna hated it. She didn't want any of his hoeish ways rubbing off on him. They'd been through enough. She didn't need any added stress in her life.

"Yeah." Tyreik reached inside his jacket pocket.

He placed a wad of cash, his phone and a lighter on the table. Tyreik handed Kingston the lighter and placed the cash back inside his pocket.

"I'm so happy y'all came tonight." Chyna said to Asia and Jaylen as she sat on the couch. "I missed my friends."

"I missed you too, friend." Asia poked out her bottom lip.

"Y'all should come to our next game at the end of the week?" Jaylen said sitting next to his wife.

"Where y'all playing? In Chicago?" Chyna asked.

"Yeah."

"I wish we could but India has to be back to school the day after tomorrow."

"I can't believe India is thirteen-years-old. She was just a freakin' baby." Asia shook her head in disbelief.

"I know. She's getting little boobies and everything."

"Oh my God," Asia laughed.

"TMI! I don't need to know that." Jaylen placed his index finger inside his ear.

"Oh hush. It's a part of life." Chyna waved him off as she noticed Tyreik's iPhone light up.

His back was turned so he didn't even see it going off. Chyna looked down at the screen. He'd received a text message that read:

<Messages   **R**   Details

I'm home... Where r u

Chyna jerked her head back and furrowed her brows. Although she didn't know who the caller was, something about the message didn't sit well in her spirit. Tyreik no longer sold work so nobody had any business texting him after midnight. Plus, the text message just reeked of a female. Reacting off instinct, Chyna hurried and pulled out her phone. Quickly, she saved the number to her contacts. With the number saved, she picked up Tyreik's phone.

"Excuse me." She stepped past her friends with an attitude.

Asia and Brooke could tell that something was wrong by the look on her face.

Stay calm, Chyna, she told herself as she walked over to Tyreik. *Don't overreact.*

"Baby!" She tapped him on the shoulder.

"What's up?" He turned around puffing on a cigar.

"Who the fuck is this?" Chyna held the phone up in his face.

So much for not overreacting, she thought.

Tyreik read the message and rolled his eyes.

"That's my homeboy Rob." He took his phone from her hand and slipped it back inside his pocket. "He told me to hit him and let him know what we was on tonight."

"Mmm hmm." Chyna pursed her lips together.

Although Tyreik had kept a straight face during his explanation, she still didn't believe him.

"Mmm hmm my ass." He shot back.

"Let me find out you cheatin' again." She squinted her eyes.

"Here you go wit' that shit. When you gon' stop bringing up the past? And what the hell you doing lookin' at my phone anyway? Yo' nosey-ass gon' get enough of that shit."

"Nah, you be on that bullshit and you know it."

"C'mon, man; chill. You ruining my vibe. It's a brand new year. Let's not start off arguing. We did enough of that last year," Tyreik pleaded.

Chyna inhaled deep and crossed her arms across her chest. Everything in her wanted to press the issue but

Tyreik was right. Now was not the time to start a war. Tyreik said it was his friend hittin' him up and she had to believe him.

If they were going to make things work and be together, she had to stop letting his past fuck ups play a role in their present. She had to trust him but trusting Tyreik had become increasingly hard over the years. He'd slung her heart through the mud. It was now covered in filth, shit and grime. Tyreik saw the doubt in her eyes. He had to take her mind off the demons that were plaguing her mind.

"Stop acting like a fuckin' brat. You know you not mad for real." He unfolded her arms and made her hug him.

Chyna reluctantly held him close.

"Gimme a kiss," he demanded.

Chyna stood on her tippy toes and planted a kiss on his lips.

"When we get home, I'm fuckin' the shit outta you." Tyreik slapped her hard on the ass.

"Fuck waitin' till we get home. Meet me in the bathroom in five minutes." She winked her eye.

"ALL MY FRIENDS SAY I CAN DO BETTER THAN YOU."

-MISSY ELLIOT FEAT. 702, BEEP ME 911

CHAPTER 2

The Hardshell Café was a snug restaurant in the heart of Soulard that featured seafood & Cajun eats in a functional, brick-walled space. It was Chyna, Brooke and Asia's favorite restaurant to go to as a group. The drinks were on point and the food was great. Chyna lived for their potato boats and Oysters Rockefeller. The restaurant was packed. People stood by the bar chugging down beers and shots. The girls sat next to the huge aquarium by the door eating, drinking and catching up.

"I hate when I come home," Asia pouted. "'Cause when it's time to leave, I never want to."

"Yeah, we miss having you around. I hate that I have to see my godson grow up on Instagram," Chyna teased.

"I hate it too but before you know it, it'll be the off-season and I'll be here again for the summer!" Asia clapped her hands with glee.

"I can't wait till it gets hot. Me and wintertime don't mix." Chyna shivered rubbing her arms.

"Now what's going on wit' you, Brooke? You and Amir still over there playin' house?" Asia arched her brow.

"Amir my boo for life. You know I ain't never leaving him. Now do I have a few friends on the side?Yes." Brooke shot her a sly grin. "You know me. I'll never be faithful to a man."

"A few friends? More like a roster. This bitch stay wit' a new nigga." Chyna cracked up laughing.

"I sure do. These niggas ain't talkin' bout shit now-a-days. All they wanna do is watch Netflix and chill. So I'ma use 'em for what they good for: some dick and some cash. A nigga can't even look my way if he ain't talkin' about giving up no dough," Brooke stressed.

"So you don't ever see yourself settling down and having a family?" Asia asked somewhat sad.

"Maybe one day." Brooke shrugged.

"Shit, you act like you young." Chyna looked at her like she was crazy. "Bitch, we almost pushing forty. By the time you decide to have kids all yo' eggs gon' be fried and gone," she joked.

"Fuck you!" Brooke giggled throwing her napkin at her. "And lies you tell. My doctor told me I have a vagina of a twenty-year-old." Brooke posed like a model.

"Girl, who she think she foolin'?" Chyna looked at Asia.

"Whatever; me and my eggs are good. But what's up wit' you and Tyreik? I saw things get a little tense between y'all on New Year's Eve."

"We good," Chyna told a half-truth.

They were doing ok but the text message kept replaying in her mind. Something about it just didn't feel right. No matter how hard she tried to push the thought away it kept on coming back.

"I mean, you know shit between me and Tyreik ain't perfect but we're working on things. We've come a long way over the years. Do we still have a long way to go? Yes. But with time, we'll get better. Everybody can't have a picture perfect relationship like Hov & Bey."

"And even them niggas ain't perfect," Brooke scoffed. "Trust and believe Beyoncé be checkin' that nigga on the regular. They ass probably stay into it but the thing is, we'll never know about it. That's how a relationship is supposed to be. Keep y'all business between y'all. The world don't need to know every time yo' dude make you mad."

"Me and Jaylen have had our fair share of ups and downs," Asia chimed in. "But I don't come running to y'all with every little thing that goes wrong between us,' cause guess what? When you constantly tell people the bad stuff that happens in your relationship, that's all they're gonna remember."

"Well, I guess that's why y'all don't like Tyreik 'cause I'm always runnin' and tellin' y'all shit." Chyna chuckled taking a sip of her drink.

"It's not that we don't like Tyreik. We just know that you can do better." Asia reached over and held her friend's hand.

"No," Brooke shook her head. "Fuck that. Tell the truth and shame the devil. Keep it one hundred. We don't like that nigga."

"Tell me how you really feel!" Chyna replied sarcastically.

"Hell, we talkin' so I'ma keep it real. You been with this nigga for how many years? Y'all still ain't married. Y'all ain't got no kids together… amen," Brooke thanked God. "Y'all forever breakin' up and makin' up. He stay on some bullshit. He's a liar. I mean, I can go on but I don't wanna hurt your feelings." She fluttered her lashes and wrapped her lips around her straw.

The alcohol in her system was taking over.

"Oh, you've said enough." Chyna situated herself in her seat.

She tried to act unfazed but Brooke's words were eating at her core. Tyreik was all of the things she said and more. Yes, he was a handful but Chyna couldn't deny all of the great qualities about him either. Her friends didn't see how when they lie in bed at night he couldn't fall asleep without holding her. They weren't there when he helped India with her homework.

Even though Chyna was at home all day, Tyreik still found the time to cook dinner for them. He was her biggest supporter when it came to her career. He was her constant source of inspiration. Sure, they were known for having catastrophic blow ups but it was the everyday, little things that kept her coming back for more.

"I'm sorry, friend. Did I say too much?" Brooke asked genuinely worried.

She knew Chyna like she knew the back of her hand. Chyna would never say it but her feelings were hurt. Brooke felt horrible. She never wanted to upset Chyna and ruin her night.

"Nah, I'm good. It is what it is. Like Asia said, people only remember the bad stuff, so I'ma make a mental note to stop running to y'all wit' every fucked up thing that happens between us. I don't tell y'all about all the good things he does for me and India. So it's kind of my fault in a way. Tyreik ain't a bad dude. He's just fucked up but so am I." She laughed off her sadness.

"You got that right. Yo' ass is crazy as hell." Brooke held up her hand for a high-five.

"You smell like Craigslist." Chyna grimaced. "I will not high-five that bullshit." She eventually laughed.

"Oooh… y'all listen to what they playin'." Asia said excitedly.

Chyna and Brooke stopped talking and listened closely. Mariah Carey's *Always Be My Baby* was playing. It was their song. Every time they heard it, it reminded them of when they were kids and Mariah Carey was Brooke's idol. The girls instantly rose to their feet and began singing the song at the top of their lungs.

"You'll always be apart of me. I'm part of you indefinitely. Boy, don't you know you can't escape me. Oooh darling 'cause you'll always be my baby." They all wrapped their arms around one another and danced from side-to-side.

The girls were so amped that other people in the restaurant started to sing along with them.

*"Yooooooooou and I... will al...ways beeeeeeeeee... Yooooooooooou and I... You and I!!"*Chyna looked her friends square in the eyes and hugged them tight.

The words to the song spoke volumes about their friendship together. No, they didn't always agree. Yes, sometimes they fought. Time sometimes elapsed where they didn't speak but that was apart of life. They'd found a sisterhood in one another that could never be replaced.

Despite life's hardships, Brooke, Asia and Chyna would always be there for one another. Men would come and go but their friendship would stand the test of time.

"YOU PROBABLY AT HOME CALLIN' ONE OF YO' BITCHES."

-CHRISS ZOE, TWERKIN' IN MY HEELS

CHAPTER 3

Sparks of fire crackled as the fireplace roared. It was a cold 25 degrees outside. Chyna lay cozy on the couch in her sitting room. The lights were dimmed low. She was dressed in her cutest pajama set and her warmest pair of socks. A cream and white Hermes blanket was up to her neck.

Chyna loved her home. She'd been living in the Soulard area of St. Louis for four years. She absolutely adored her neighborhood. During the week it was quiet but on the weekends it was turn up time. Dozens of restaurants and bars lined the streets. There was always something to do. Chyna never lacked entertainment.

She and Tyreik originally got the 3-story townhome together at the end of 2009 but in 2011, after a horrific fight, Tyreik and Chyna broke up. He moved into his own spot. Chyna re-signed the lease in her name and redecorated the house to suit her taste. After a few months, the two were back together. Tyreik moved back in and all was forgiven.

He hated the girly décor but had no choice but to tolerate it since he no longer had a say so. Chyna's entire home had a Forever 21, Urban Outfitters feel to it. It was very eclectic and artsy. The constant theme throughout the home were the colors black and white with pops of pink. The sitting room was no different.

A white, four paneled, glass cabinet with Chyna's books and awards rested against the black and white wall. A body-hugging, white sectional with pink and grey throw pillows took up half the room. In front of the sectional was a black coffee table. A biography on Elizabeth Taylor, a vase filled with fresh flowers and candles decorated the table. A 50 inch flat screen hung from the wall above the fireplace.

Chyna loved nights like this. It was family movie night. India, her 13-year-old daughter, got to pick the movies of course. India lie on the plush carpeted floor dressed in her PJs as well. Chyna took a moment to take in her daughter. Looking at India was like staring into the mirror. She had the same honey-colored skin, big, doe-shaped eyes and pouty, kissable lips as her mother.

Her wild, curly hair hung past her shoulders. When she smiled, a set of deep dimples popped out like the sun. She was the cutest thirteen-year-old Chyna had ever seen. Many people told her she looked like Amandla Stenberg.

India was Chyna's prized possession and greatest accomplishment in life. Chyna had done a few things in life right and one of them was raising a beautiful, smart, respectful, funny, considerate, strong daughter. India was like her mother in a lot of ways but for the most part, she was her own person. She wasn't into fashion or boys. India cared about her studies, video games and the weather.

She was obsessed with tornados and hurricanes and had expressed on several occasions that she planned on being a meteorologist or video game creator. Chyna was just happy that her daughter wasn't out in the streets being hot like she was at her age. By the time Chyna was thirteen, she had already been finger popped by her crush on his bed.

That night they were watching The Avengers. India and Chyna loved watching superhero movies. They both were heavily into the movie but Chyna couldn't stop cutting her eyes over at Tyreik. He sat next to her in a tee shirt and jeans barely watching the film.

She couldn't help but notice that every five minutes he was picking up his phone and replying to text messages. To make it so bad, he wasn't even being discreet about it. Chyna was beyond annoyed. It was past 11:00pm on a

Friday. *Who could he possibly be texting*, she wondered. Hell, she was right there so it for damn sure wasn't her.

Niggas didn't sit up and text each other at night so that eliminated his friends. The only other person it could possibly be was a chick. With that notion in her head, Chyna didn't give a fuck about the movie anymore. She wanted to know what the hell he was doing. Staring at him, she shot him a death glare. Tyreik could feel her eyes boring into his skin. He immediately stopped texting and glanced over at her.

"Is there a problem?" He asked matter-of-factly.

"Yeah, what are you doing?" She spoke in a low tone so she wouldn't disturb India.

"What does it look like I'm doing?" Tyreik said in a low tone back.

"Don't get smart with me. I know exactly what you're doing. Who are you textin' this time of night?" Chyna's nostrils flared.

"I'm handling business; do you mind?" Tyreik screwed up his face.

"Actually, I do 'cause we're supposed to be spending family time together. So put your phone up please." She flashed a quick smile then went back to being stone faced.

"I will when I get done taking care of this." Tyreik went back to texting.

Chyna stared at him for a long while before rolling her eyes. He had her entire life fucked up.

"Ay, I'ma need your help with rent this month. My check still ain't came," she said.

"I'll have to see what I can do."

"What you mean? You just got paid for the New Year's Eve party."

"And I had some things I needed to take care of." He remarked becoming mad.

Chyna sat confused. *What things do he have to take care of*, she thought. His car was paid for. He didn't have any car insurance. All this nigga had was his cell phone bill.

"Well, I'ma need yo' help so you gon' have to figure it out."

"A'ight." Tyriek replied, concentrating on his text conversation.

The fact that he hadn't stopped got under Chyna's skin. Each time he tapped his fingers on the screen she wanted to rip the phone from his hands and throw it across the room.

"If you ain't gon' watch the movie, then why are you even in here?" Her temper flared.

"I told you to give me a minute, damn." Tyreik huffed hitting the send button. "There, I'm done. You happy now?" He placed his phone face down on the arm of the couch.

"As a matter-of-fact, I am." Chyna smirked, pleased she'd gotten her way.

Although she'd gotten him to stop textin', that didn't take away the fact that he'd placed his phone face down. Chyna peeped everything. Inhaling deep, she tried to calm her sneaky suspensions but something just wasn't right. She'd been here one too many times with Tyreik. Her female intuition was telling her he was up to no good.

She didn't want to believe it because they'd been doing so well. He was home every night with her. But Chyna was too smart for that bullshit. Just because a muthafucka came home every night didn't mean he couldn't find time to cheat. She knew how the game was played. She'd been a cheater once before herself.

Tyreik was hot. Chicks stayed throwing the pussy at him but he'd committed over ten years of his life to her. That had to count for something. Chyna just couldn't go through the drama of finding out he was cheating again. When he'd cheated in the past with Rema, it was almost too much for her to bear. It damn near killed her.

Chyna wasn't an angel. She'd done her fair share of dirt over the years. But she was no longer the wide-eyed, bushy tale girl he'd met at 16. The shit he pulled back then wouldn't fly now. She was a 31-year-old woman with needs and demands. And sure, underneath her pretty face lie a world of trouble.

Chyna was insecure and distrustful of everything. Her attitude went from 0 to 100 real quick. When you pissed her off, she tried her best to kill you with her words. She was petty and vengeful but Tyreik had made her this way. He'd turned her into a jealous, anxious, unsure of herself monster. She'd forgiven Tyreik for cheating on her in the past but truthfully, she'd never gotten over it.

The scar still remained etched deep into her heart. She wanted desperately to believe that her mind was playing tricks on her but the signs of betrayal were all there. Chyna couldn't allow herself to be played out again. Doubt swarmed her head. She couldn't lie next to Tyreik one more night without knowing the truth.

"I THOUGHT WE WERE PAST THESE GAMES."

-JAZMINE SULLIVAN FEAT. MEEK MILL, DUMB

CHAPTER 4

The following night, Chyna sat on her laptop editing a makeup tutorial for her YouTube channel, Color Me Pynk. After years of dying to have her own channel, Chyna finally bit the bullet and started filming. To her surprise, Color Me Pynk was getting good feedback. The viewership wasn't where she wanted it yet but she'd just gotten started and had time to grow.

Chyna and Tyreik had the whole house to themselves. India was gone for the night at her Grandmother Diane's house. Instead of spending the night at home with Chyna, Tyreik made plans to kick it with his homeboys. Chyna didn't care that he was hitting the streets. She had business of her own that needed tending to.

Tyriek stood in front of the full-length mirror situating his outfit to his liking. Chyna cut her eyes at him. Tyreik didn't have much but he always made sure he looked good. He spent all of his money on clothes and shoes. He was the flyest bum she'd ever seen. Chyna hated that he was still so damn fine. Clothes framed him so well. Tyreik wasn't even wearing anything spectacular. It was his swag that made his fit so fly.

He donned an Alexander McQueen, black, bomber jacket, his favorite gold, Cuban link chain tucked inside a white Yeezus, oversized tank top, distressed jeans and Bathing Ape, special edition Converse, graffiti sneakers.

"You cute," she remarked.

"Thanks." Tyreik sprayed himself with Dolce & Gabbana Velvet Bergamot cologne.

Just the scent of the cologne made Chyna want to rip his clothes off and take him right there on the floor. However, leading with her vagina and not her head was what had her in the predicament she was in.

"You figured out what you gon' do as far as the rent goes?"

"No, I haven't. I'll figure out something," Tyreik replied annoyed.

"Where y'all going?" Chyna died to know.

"We heading over to Juelz's crib to watch the fight. He having a few people over."

"Mmm... sounds like fun. It's gon' be some hoes over there?" She quizzed.

"I don't know who that man got coming over." Tyreik exclaimed surprised by her line of questioning.

"Sure you don't." Chyna replied under her breath.

"I heard that." Tyreik said over his shoulder.

"Good."

"Stop." He walked over and kissed her cheek. "I'm about to head out. I'll call you when I get there."

"Have fun." Chyna responded dryly as he left out the door.

As soon as he pulled out of the driveway it was as if a switch went off in her mind. It was now or never. If she wanted to quiet her doubts she had to call the number and see who answered. She knew that by calling the number she would be opening Pandora's Box. Everything about their relationship could possibly change afterwards.

But if she let it go, the suspicion would always be there. It would gnaw at her. Unsure of what she should do, Chyna paced back and forth across her bedroom floor. If she kept it up she would spark a fire. She was a nervous wreck. A million butterflies filled her stomach.

"Ok, fuck it." She picked up her phone. "I'ma call."

Chyna located the number in her contacts and stared at it for what seemed like hours. A rush of anxiety washed over her. This was it.

"Lord, please let a man answer." She prayed, as she pressed *67 and dialed the number.

Her palms were sweaty as hell as the phone started to ring. For a second she thought no one was going to answer but by the fifth ring someone picked up.

"Hello?" A woman answered cautiously.

Chyna's heart instantly sank down to her toes. She just knew that it was going to be a dude that answered the phone but it wasn't. She knew that voice from anywhere. It haunted her in her sleep. She hadn't heard the voice in years but she was almost sure it was her arch-enemy.

"Helllooo?" The woman said again.

"Umm." Chyna cleared her throat. "I'm sorry; is Rob there?"

"You have the wrong number." The woman hung up.

Chyna held the phone up to her ear and willed the tears in her eyes not to fall. *Pull it together, bitch. You don't even know for sure if it was her,* she tried to convince herself. *Who you foolin', Chyna? You know damn well it was her.* Needing to get to the bottom of things, she called Asia.

Brooke was the person she should've been calling. She was the person you called when you needed answers to anything ratchet. Brooke always had her ear to the streets. She stayed on top of game. But Chyna didn't feel like hearing a bunch of "I told you so's, that nigga ain't shit, fuck him, you need to leave him alone" advice She needed to vent and not be judged. Asia was the perfect person to go to for that. She was rational and made it easy for Chyna to express herself.

"Please be home." She said a silent prayer to God as her leg shook violently.

"What up, ho?" Asia finally answered.

"What you doing?" Chyna's voice trembled.

"Just got done putting the baby to sleep. Why, what's up? What's wrong wit' you?" Asia asked hearing the strain in her voice.

"I gotta tell you something and when I do I don't wanna hear a bunch of shit. Just listen and help."

"A'ight, damn, bitch." Asia said taken aback by her friend's abrupt behavior.

"Ok listen, you remember on New Year's Eve when we were at the club? We was sittin' on the couch talkin' and I got up and went over to Tyreik with an attitude?"

"Yeah."

"Ok, well the reason I was mad was because Tyreik got a text from somebody name R that said 'I'm home, where are you?'. Well, that threw me for a loop because Tyreik don't be on the phone like that and street dudes don't text that late at night, so I immediately got on this nigga got me fucked up alert. I saved the number to my phone then asked him about it. He said that R was his pot'nah Rob. I ain't believe him but decided not to press the issue."

"Ok," Asia listened closely.

"Well, last night, we were having family movie night and it's going on midnight and this big head muthafucka is on his phone textin'. I asked him who he was talkin' to. He said he was taking care of business. Now obviously this nigga think I'm Boo-Boo the Fool 'cause I ain't believe that shit either."

"You stupid," Asia couldn't help but laugh.

"So, long story short, Tyreik just left. I had to call the number to see if he was tellin' the truth or not." Chyna said at once.

"Oh Lord," Asia sighed, dreading what she was about to hear next.

"Yeah...oh Lord." Chyna repeated.

"A girl answered the phone." Asia took a wild guess.

"You know it. I asked to speak to Rob and she said I had the wrong number."

"Damn." Asia shook her head.

"Nah, but catch this tea. On my life I think the girl was Rema."

"Get the fuck outta here," Asia replied genuinely shocked.

Hearing Rema's name was the equivalent to seeing a zombie in a horror flick rise from the dead.

"Why you think that?"

"'Cause I know that bitch voice," Chyna declared, rolling her eyes.

"Now what?" Asia questioned unfazed by the content of the conversation.

"I want you to call the number back and ask to speak to Rema," Chyna said amped.

"Absolutely not."

"Why not?" Chyna whined.

"'Cause we've been down this road before, girl. You already know what it is."

"I just need confirmation," Chyna pleaded.

"You already got confirmation when you dialed the number the first time. I love you, friend, but this shit is ridiculous. And I know you asked me not to say nothing but I have to. Chyna, you and Tyreik been doing this dumb shit for how many years? Bitch, you damn near forty and still callin' hoes to see if they fuckin' yo' nigga. That shit ain't cute no more. That shit is borderline pathetic."

Chyna listened to her friend scold her with a huge lump in her throat. She knew she sounded dumb as fuck but she couldn't help herself. Despite all the shit Tyreik took her through, she still held out hope that one day he'd change. He'd made so many strides through the years. Once he got this other shit under control, they'd be solid as a rock.

"You Chyna Black, bitch. You better start acting like it," Asia said with a sudden fierceness.

"You got all this shit going for you and this is the only thing holding you back from taking you to the next level. Tyreik is a hindrance to you, honey. When y'all into it you can't write. You're not focused. Nothing gets done and you and Tyreik fight way too much for that shit. So I'ma say this to you. If you need more proof, call her back yourself. And don't take me saying no as I don't' love you 'cause I do."

"I know you do," Chyna sniffed, wiping away her tears.

"If you wanna be a wife like me, then you have to stop tolerating bullshit and realize that you deserve better," Asia reasoned.

"I know you think I'm stupid and I probably am but I gotta find out if it was her." Chyna said unwilling to leave well enough alone.

"This is a no judgment zone, honey. I got yo' back regardless," Asia assured.

"Thanks. I'ma call you back in a minute."

"A'ight, let me know what happens." Asia ended the call.

Done with playing games, Chyna dialed the number once more. This time the woman answered on the first ring.

"Hello?" She answered with an attitude.

"Speak to Rema?"

"This me. Who is this?" Rema asked taken aback.

Chyna closed her eyes and counted to ten. *This can't be happening.* She thought she'd never be in this place again. Yet here she was. *This muthafucka still ain't shit,* she massaged her forehead.

"Hello? Who is this?" Rema said angrily.

"Rema, this is Chyna," Chyna responded back wryly.

"Why are you callin' my phone and how did you get my number?"

"'Cause I need to ask you a question. Are you and Tyreik back fuckin' around?" Chyna asked matter-of-factly.

By posing the question she knew she was placing herself in a vulnerable space. She was willingly putting herself in a position to be played. Rema laughed a bit. Chyna furrowed her brows pissed.

"That's something you need to ask him and don't call my phone no more." She said before hanging up in Chyna's ear.

Chyna's head began to spin. Here she was again back at Ground Zero. She couldn't believe Tyreik had the audacity to put her in the same position for the umpteenth time and with a bitch he knew she couldn't stand. He'd looked her in the eyes and swore never to see or speak to Rema again.

He didn't even respect Chyna enough to do the shit in private. He blatantly texted the ho in her face like she was stupid. Maybe Chyna was dumb. She'd given half of her life to a lying sack of shit who only cared about himself. He didn't give a fuck about her. How could he when he continuously did shit like this to hurt her?

Chyna sat on the edge of the bed drowning in tears. Her heart had shattered into a million pieces. For the life of her she couldn't understand how someone who claimed to love her could do so much fucked up shit. Was it all a game to him? 'Cause she was obviously losing.

Once more, he'd given her the kiss of death. Chyna had died a million times behind Tyreik and his lies. She couldn't allow him to do her like this ever again. Quickly, her sorrow vanished and was replaced with seething anger.

"This muthafucka gon' text that bitch in my face? Oh word? Ok, I got something for his ass." She shot up from the bed and began to snatch his clothes off the hangers.

He wouldn't be spending another night there. Chyna viciously threw his clothes over her shoulder while spewing words of hate. Once the majority of his clothes were sprawled on the floor, she wiped the sweat from her brow and called him. Tyreik answered on the second ring.

"What's up, baby?" He said cheerfully.

Chyna could hear a lot of people in the background. She specifically zeroed in on a slew of female voices which pissed her off even more.

"Come get yo' shit."

"What?" Tyreik screwed up his face confused.

"You heard me. Come get your shit before I sit it outside." Chyna advised not playing games.

"Hold up." Tyreik walked out of the room so he could hear her better. "Who pissed in your cereal? What's wrong wit' you?"

"You're what's wrong with me! You must think I'm so stupid, don't you?" Chyna bobbed her head back and forth. "I called the number, asshole! You know, the one you said was your homeboy Rob's number! You lied to me! That was Rema's number, nigga! So you back on that bullshit, huh?"

Tyreik damn near dropped his phone. He never expected to hear her say that. He thought he'd covered all shit tracks.

"Chyna, nah... I don't even... man." Tyreik tried to find the words to say but couldn't.

"Cat got yo' tongue? Talk, nigga! You was bold enough to cheat; be bold enough to confess to the shit! Nah, fuck that! You ain't gotta explain shit to me. Just come get ya' shit and get the fuck out!" Chyna hung up feeling stronger than ever before.

"THEY DON'T WANNA SEE YOU HAPPIER THAN THEM."

-BEYONCÉ FEAT. DRAKE, MINE

CHAPTER 5

Thirty minutes didn't even go by before Tyreik came bursting through the door. He found Chyna sitting at the head of the bed with her knees up to her chest. Dried tears stained her face. He felt like shit for causing her to cry but all of that went out of the window when he saw his designer clothes crumpled up on the floor.

"What the fuck are you doing?" He picked his things up off the floor one by one. "This is Alexander Wang and Givenchy! You don't do that." He sat his clothes on the bed.

"Get that shit off my bed!" Chyna kicked them right back off again.

"Baby." Tyreik tried to come near her.

"You bet not touch me." Chyna pointed her finger at him.

"Damn, will you just listen?" He sat next to her. "I don't know what that bitch told you but she lyin'. I ain't fuckin' wit' that girl," he pleaded.

Tyreik was going to do or say whatever he needed to in order not to lose Chyna.

"That girl ain't lyin'. You the one lyin'."

"So you gon' believe her over me? She don't even like you."

"I don't give a fuck about that bitch not liking me!" Chyna shouted getting in his face. "And if that bitch don't like me then why the fuck you talkin' to her?" She mushed him in the forehead.

Knowing she had a point, Tyreik tried to think of a response.

"Ain't no point of me even tryin' to explain myself. You gon' believe what you wanna believe anyway." He waved her off.

"I believe you ain't shit! How 'bout that? So get your shit and get yo' lousy-ass the fuck out my house!" She shoved him forcefully.

"C'mon, man, stop!" Tyreik grabbed her wrist and held her close.

He could feel her chest heave up and down frantically.

"Don't let something some hatin' ass bitch tell you tear us apart. We've been doing good, babe," he said desperately.

"Let me go, Tyriek." Chyna asked calmly.

"Not until you calm down and listen."

"I ain't listening to shit you got to say 'cause when I asked you for the truth, you lied!" Chyna broke loose and hit him in the arm.

"Here I am giving you everything I have and you still doing the same shit you was doing back in '97. You too old for this shit! Grow the fuck up!" She swung her arms wildly.

"I told you I ain't do shit!" Tyreik grabbed her again and pushed her down onto the bed.

With her arms in his grasp, he restrained her from hitting him.

"I called the bitch phone, Tyreik! Stop lying'!" Chyna kicked and screamed.

"I'm not fuckin' lyin'!" He shook her.

"Yes you are!"

"Man, whatever." He pushed her hands away fed up. "Believe what you wanna believe. I don't even give a fuck." He shot dismissively.

Chyna sat up and cried. Her heart was on E. She felt like at any moment she was going to die.

"My friends were right. I need to leave yo' ass alone."

"Your friends?" Tyreik turned around and mean mugged her. "Your friends are some fuckin' haters. Them hoes can't tell you shit, especially not Brooke," he exclaimed.

"She stay cheatin'. Every nigga in St. Louis done had her! And the only reason Asia wit' Jaylen is because you ain't want him! So don't tell me shit about what your friends say! They opinion don't mean shit to me! They don't wanna see you happier than them no way," he barked.

Chyna had him completely fucked up if she thought she was going to hit him with that logic.

"Don't talk about my friends. You just mad 'cause they spoke the truth about yo' ass."

Chyna paused and continued to sob.

"I'm so sick of cryin' behind you. I don't know what to do." She cried so hard her chest ached.

"You ain't gotta worry about it no more." Tyreik started to pack up some of his things.

"So you not gon' even say sorry? You just gon' act like the shit ain't happen, like you ain't do nothin'? You gon' play me like I'm crazy for real?" She asked stunned.

"You are fuckin' crazy! You fuckin' nuts! I told you I'm not fuckin' that bitch! I ain't gotta put up with this shit." Tyreik threw his things in a Louis Vuitton duffle bag. "Believe what you wanna believe."

"Fuck you!" Chyna hopped off the bed and got up in his face. "I ain't gotta put up with this shit either! I don't need you!"

"Exactly and fuck you too." Tyreik shot sarcastically. "Every time something pop off the first thing you wanna do is accuse somebody of cheatin' and threaten to put 'em out. You act like you live in Trump Towers.

Fuck you and this house. I get tired of that shit." He pulled his underwear and socks from out of the drawer.

"Whatever, Tyreik, just go and give me back my damn key." Chyna held her hand out.

"You can have this muthafuckin' key." Tyreik took the key off his keychain and threw it at her. "I'm out this bitch, but when you realize you overreacted, don't come callin' me cryin' like you always do."

"Trust and believe I won't." Chyna replied, feeling the air in her lungs disappear.

"Yeah ok, that's what yo' mouth say," Tyreik smirked. "In a few days you gon' be callin' me beggin' me to come back. But I got something for yo' ass. It'll be a cold day in hell before I step foot in this muthafucka again."

The thought of Tyreik leaving and never coming back again made Chyna feel sick to her stomach but she couldn't let him know that.

"Fuck you!" He zipped up his bag.

"Fuck me?" Chyna felt like she'd been shot point blank in the heart.

He'd cheated on her but somehow she was the one to blame.

"Fuck me?" She repeated. "No, nigga! Fuck you! You stupid muthafucka! You think I can't get nobody else? I can do ten times better than you! Niggas try to get at me all the time but noooooo here I am stuck on stupid behind yo' broke ass!"

"Now I'm a broke-ass nigga? I wasn't broke when I was buying you Fendi, Gucci and Chanel! You the stupid one. Sitting up here takin' a bitch word that don't even like you over mine. And you can stop actin' like you Miss Goody Two-Shoes! Yo' ass ain't fuckin' innocent. Let's not forget when you fucked my homeboy!" Tyreik yelled swiping her laptop off the bed.

It landed loudly with a thud on the hardwood floor. Seeing red, he took his foot and stomped the top of it. Chyna gasped in fear. She couldn't believe that he'd done such a thing. Her laptop was her livelihood. If he broke her laptop she wouldn't be able to write.

"Why would you do that?" She said in disbelief.

Tyreik immediately realized that what he'd done was wrong but he was so enraged he didn't care.

"I'm out." He stormed out of the room without saying sorry.

Chyna dropped to her knees and picked up her laptop. She prayed it still worked. Tyreik had stomped it so hard that there was a huge footprint on the face. She tried to power it back on but the screen stayed black. Utterly devastated, she sat in a heap of tears on the floor.

"LOVES THE DRAMA SHE CHOSE IT."

-G-EAZY, TUMBLR GIRLS

CHAPTER 6

Chyna lie in bed unable to feel her heart. Silence surrounded her. The only sound that could be heard was the sound of her tears hitting the pillowcase. She could barely see through the tears in her eyes. She'd done nothing but cry since Tyreik left. She was so tired of him toying with her emotions. If he loved her as much as he said he did, then why couldn't he act right?

Everything with him was a constant battle. Just when she thought they were on the path to greatness, he went and did something stupid to fuck it up again. It made her feel like everything he said was a lie. He couldn't possibly love her the way he said he did. She couldn't take being constantly mind-fucked by him.

Wasn't he tired of seeing her cry? He had to be as tired as she was. She was mentally and physically exhausted by him and his selfish-ass ways. If she did half the shit he did, he would've been left. He wouldn't be able to handle it. When she'd betrayed his trust in the past he'd lost his shit and damn near tried to kill her.

Chyna knew that after this betrayal she had to be done. She'd be a fool to stay after this. She was 31-years-old. Enough was enough. But try telling that to the never-ending ache in her chest. Sometimes it felt like dealing with Tyreik and his bullshit was easier than being without him. The pain of not having him around was unbearable. She hadn't been able to move a muscle.

She hated when she got like this. Being without him literally made her feel physically ill. Eating or sleeping wasn't an option. Mourning his latest indiscretion had fully taken over her everyday routine. For days she did nothing but study the crevices in the wall. She wouldn't even answer the phone for her friends. She didn't want them to find out. She couldn't take the risk of looking even dumber in their eyes.

Everything they said about Tyreik was spot on. He was selfish, manipulative, a liar, inconsiderate, mean, lazy and down right cruel. During moments like these, Chyna wondered how she actually thought they could make it. Had she been on dope? Was she getting high off her own supply? Or was she strictly high off of him?

Being with him made her feel wanted. She would do anything to keep him around. She'd give up everything she owned for him. No one could understand the effect he had on her. It was sick how bad she was stuck on him.

From the moment they met, there was an unexplainable, gravitational pull between them. She felt it in her gut every time she was in his presence.

When they were together nothing mattered but him and her. She was the Bonnie to his Clyde, the Kim to his Kanye. Together they could take over the world. If they ever broke up for good she wouldn't be able to go on. Chyna needed Tyreik like she needed air to breathe. The touch of his hand calmed her fears.

The sound of his deep voice soothed her ears. He was the only man that knew how to control her. She felt small in his presence, like a little girl. And when they made love, time stood still. Tyreik's dick was made especially for her. She wasn't ashamed to admit she was dickmitized.

His stroke game was mind-blowing. He knew exactly how to please her. With him, she was completely inhibited. Over the years, he had her doing things she thought she'd never do. Chyna would do any and everything to please him. He was her baby. He'd been there for her when things got rough.

One Christmas she'd gotten stiffed by one of her publishers on her royalty check and Tyreik went and bought all of India's Christmas gifts. Without him, she didn't know what she would've done. Christmas would've been ruined if it wasn't for him. It was moments like that that made her fall in love with him all over again.

Besides that, Chyna wasn't trying to start over. Getting back into the dating field wasn't appealing to her. She'd heard the horror stories and wanted no parts of it. She'd stuck it out this long with Tyreik. Why give up now? He'd get it together sooner than later and they'd be able to ride off into the sunset.

Staring at the wall, she allowed the tears to fall freely from her swollen eyes. She didn't know if she was madder at the fact he'd cheated or that she still wanted him. All she'd did was catch them talkin'. *That didn't mean they were having a full-fledged affair,* she tried to convince herself. Whether they were smashing or not was irrelevant.

He had no business communicating with the funky bitch. She was Chyna's arch-enemy. She despised the ho. But Chyna couldn't even be mad at Rema. Hoes were gonna be hoes and ho-ass niggas like Tyreik were only gon' do what muthafucka's allowed him to do. She couldn't spend another year of her life policing a grown-ass man. If he wanted to be single, then he could easily walk out the door.

She didn't need him. He needed her. That didn't change the fact that she still wanted him and he wanted her too. If he didn't he wouldn't have kept running back to her. He'd been calling non-stop since she put him out. Chyna didn't bother to answer his calls or his texts. She wanted to make him suffer. She had to keep his ass on his toes.

"Mom," India tapped on her door.

Chyna hurried and wiped her tears away. She knew it wouldn't help much. She was sure India had heard her crying. Plus, it was the middle of the day and she was still in bed which wasn't like her at all. Chyna sat up and looked at her daughter. India had just got out of school. She was still dressed in her uniform.

"Yes, baby."

"Mom, what's wrong?"

"Nothing. I'm just not feeling good." Chyna told half the truth.

"You want me to fix you something to eat? You haven't eaten in days." India asked genuinely concerned for her mother's well-being.

"You're such a sweet girl." Chyna caressed the side of India's face. "I'm good."

"Where is Tyreik?" India looked around. "Why hasn't he been here?"

"We got into it and I made him leave." Chyna replied honestly.

She always tried to keep it one hundred with her daughter.

"He's not coming back?" India asked hopeful.

"No, not this time." Chyna lied to her daughter and herself. "But enough of that. You got homework?"

"Yeah." India wiped a tear from the corner of her mother's eye.

"Go do your homework and when you're done, I'll fix dinner. We'll eat and watch TV together. Ok?" Chyna tried to fake being happy.

"Ok." India got up from the bed.

She didn't want to leave her mother but didn't want to disobey her by staying either. Reluctantly, she left the room. India might've been young but she wasn't dumb. She knew her mother was upset over something Tyreik had done. It was the only time she became sad and depressed. The sad part about it was that India knew her mom wouldn't be happy again until he came back.

Alone again, Chyna lie back. She was a mess. She had to pull herself together if not for her sake then for India's. To her pleasure and dismay her phone started to ring. She didn't even have to look at the screen to know who it was. It was Tyreik. She had that nigga shook.

He had her fucked up if he thought she was going to break and call him first. No, it was his turn to beg for her forgiveness. She eyed the phone and wondered if she should finally pick up. Her silent treatment had lasted long enough. Now it was time to go into phase two… guilt. Chyna answered the call.

"What?" She spat with an attitude.

"Why you ain't been answering the phone? I was about to come over there," Tyreik panicked.

"No the hell you weren't. What do you want?"

"You know what I want - you. I'm sorry for the way I acted. You just pissed me off accusing me of something I'm not doing."

"If you gon' continue to lie, then we might as well end this conversation now," Chyna informed.

"I'm tellin' you the truth, babe. Ain't shit going down between me and her," Tyreik declared.

"I called her, Tyreik, and asked her verbatim are y'all fuckin' around and she said I should ask you. You know what that insinuates!"

"It insinuates a bunch of bullshit. She just tryin' to fuck wit' yo' head. I'm over here miserable as fuck and so are you and for what?"He barked.

"I ain't miserable!" Chyna played it off like she was straight. "Please believe I'm doing just fine without you. I don't know what you thought."

"Man, please. I can hear it all in yo' voice. You miss the fuck outta me. And if you don't, I miss you." Tyreik said sweetly. "Stop all the bullshit, baby. I wanna come home."

"Where you at?" Chyna asked curiously.

"I'm at Kingston crib. Shit, if you don't let me come home soon I'ma have to get a hotel room."

"I thought you ain't have no money?" Chyna quizzed.

"I got a li'l change. Why; you still need help with the rent?"

"No, my check came but you still gon' give me some money," she demanded.

"I got you," Tyreik promised.

Chyna lie quiet. She wasn't sure if she wanted Tyreik to come back just yet. She still didn't believe him and he'd acted a complete fool when he left.

"You know you broke my computer, right?"

"I did? My bad. That was fucked up. I shouldn't have did that. I'll get you another one."

"You got that right but it ain't even about that tho. Every time you get mad you wanna fuck up my shit."

"You right and I promise I won't do it again. Look, fuck all this talkin' on the phone shit. You know I don't even get down like that."

"You sholl got down like that when you was textin' that bitch in my face," Chyna countered.

"I ain't gon' even respond to that."

"Yeah, 'cause you know it's the truth." She spat getting mad all over again.

"What you doing tonight?" Tyreik changed the subject.

"I promised India I would chill with her."

"Let me take you out to dinner," Tyreik implored.

Chyna scratched her head. She knew if she came face-to-face with Tyreik that she'd break. But she couldn't quiet the yearning in her heart to see him.

"Ok, what time you picking me up?"

"WHOEVER GETS HER PUSSY THE WETTEST IS USUALLY THE LEAST GOOD FOR HER."—SOURCE UNKNOWN

CHAPTER 7

Ari Lennox's *Cascade* played loudly as Chyna sat at her vanity placing the finishing touches on her makeup look. She adored her Hollywood vanity mirror and lights. She always felt like a movie star when she got dressed. She looked fabulous to say the least. The next phase of her torture scheme was regret.

When Tyreik saw her, she wanted him to regret ever trying to play her. Her hair was flat ironed straight with a deep part in the middle. She rocked a blood red, NYX, matte lipstick on her lips. A simple pair of diamond stud earrings that Tyreik bought her when she was young gleamed from her ears. The earrings were the only jewelry she wore.

On her body was a barely there, black, block paneled, sheer dress that stopped at her knee. Underneath she wore a black, strapless bra and black panties. On her feet were her favorite black, six inch, Louboutin 'So Kate' heels. Tyreik's jaw would surely drop when he laid eyes on her. Chyna's full body was on display for the whole world to see. Whatever restaurant he was taking her to, she was sure to turn heads.

"MOM!" India shouted over the loud music.

Chyna jumped and turned around. "Girl, you scared me." She clutched her chest.

"I called your name like three times. You got the music up so loud you couldn't hear me." India turned the volume down.

She'd showered and changed into her pajamas. She was ready to spend the rest of the evening with her mother.

"You leaving?" She looked at her mom all dolled up.

"Yeah, Tyreik's taking me out to dinner," Chyna replied regrettably.

As soon as the words passed through her lips, she felt like crap.

"But I thought we were going to watch TV together? I thought you said he wasn't coming back?" India said visibly disappointed.

For the past few days her mother had locked herself in her room and shut the world out because of something Tyreik had done. She barely had a word to say to anyone, including India. Now when she decided to join the world again, she forsakes her child to spend time with the same person who'd made her cry in the first place? India didn't understand it.

"We will tomorrow. I promise and he's not coming back. Mama and Tyreik are just gonna talk." Chyna tried to believe her own lies.

India didn't even waste her energy or time on the conversation after that. She'd been here one too many times with her mother. For some odd reason her mom couldn't help but be stuck on stupid when it came to Tyreik. She was smart in every other aspect of her life except that one. It was sad because India had become accustomed to being placed to the side when it came to their relationship. Sure her mother loved her. They had an unbreakable bond but when it came to Tyreik, Chyna was a total disappointment in her daughter's eyes.

"Ok." India turned around to leave, over the conversation.

"I love you." Chyna yelled behind her feeling like shit.

"Love you too." India exhaled noisily leaving the room.

Chyna turned and looked at herself in the mirror. Although she looked stunning she hated her reflection. Everything pretty about her had instantly become ugly. A fifty pound boulder felt like it was sitting on her chest. She hated disappointing her daughter but lately that's all she'd been doing. She wanted to stop herself but couldn't. She was trapped in a never-ending maze and couldn't find her way out. *You'll make it up to her. She'll understand. She'll forgive you. But can you forgive yourself?*

Knowing the weight of the question, Chyna snapped back to reality. She inhaled deeply and placed her worries to the side. A few minutes later, Tyrcik texted her and said he was at the door. Chyna placed on her black trench coat and grabbed her Edie Parker, black, soft lava, velvet clutch. On the way to the door she stopped by India's room. India was lying on her bed watching the Disney Channel. Chyna peeked her head inside and looked around.

She wished that when she was India's age she had a room like hers. India's room was on the first floor of the house. She basically had a wing all to herself. Pink,

Chinese lanterns hung from her ceiling. A collage of pictures of India and her friends hung on the wall.

A long, white stand shelved her books, iPad, laptop and magazines. Her flat screen sat on top, opposite her custom queen size bed. India designed the bed herself. The entire unit was made so that her bed was connected to her dresser. A black and white polka dot comforter set and pink frilly pillows filled her bed.

"I'm getting ready to go," Chyna announced.

"Ok." India replied not even bothering to acknowledge her presence.

Chyna felt horrible for upsetting her daughter but she'd make it up to her. She always did.

"I'll only be gone a few hours. Have that phone by you 'cause I'ma call and check on you. You can fix you a pizza for dinner," she instructed.

"Ok." India picked up the remote and changed the channel.

"I'll be back in a minute." Chyna said once more before backing away from the doorway.

Apart of her thought about staying and keeping her promise to India but she was already dressed and ready to go. Tyreik was at the door and she was starving. She and India would spend the entire afternoon together the following day. Chyna unlocked the door and found Tyreik standing there looking sinfully delicious.

Upon sight, her nipples got hard. The waves in his hair were spinning out of control. She almost got seasick just looking at them. The sinister flicker in his eye that attracted her to him shined under the moonlight. Like her, he wore all black. He donned a black Lanvin blazer, black, slouchy tee shirt, his gold Cuban link chain, black Saint Laurent jeans and black, metallic trimmed, leather, high top sneakers. She wanted to hate him but as soon as their eyes met the ice around her heart began to thaw.

"You look pretty." He looked her up and down.

Tyreik couldn't deny Chyna's beauty if he tried. He wanted to swim in her dimples. He'd missed her terribly. Chyna simply looked at him, rolled her eyes and sauntered past him. Tyreik couldn't do anything but grin and follow her to the car. He drove a matte black, 2011 Mercedes Benz G-Class SUV. The truck was his prized possession. Outside of his clothes, it was the only thing he owned. Tyreik opened the passenger side door for Chyna and helped her in.

Chyna placed on her seat belt. She sat in silence as they drove to their destination. She and Tyreik didn't say a word to each other the whole car ride. Trey Songz's *Fumble* bumped as they coasted along the city streets. They ended up not very far from her house. The restaurant's name was Mango.

Mango provided authentic Peruvian fusion food. It was nestled downtown in the Washington Avenue loft district. Tyreik got out and opened Chyna's door. The cold, brisk wind nearly blew her over as she stepped out. She couldn't get inside the warm restaurant fast enough. Tyreik already made reservations so they were seated immediately.

At the table, Tyreik helped Chyna with her coat. He stood behind her as she unfastened her belt. The magnetic smell of her Tory Burch perfume filled his nostrils as her coat fell from her arms. Tyreik's eyes nearly popped out of its sockets when he saw what she wore. A hush fell over the entire restaurant as Chyna smoothed down her dress.

Her ass and titties were on display for the world to see. She was covered by a bra and panties but Tyreik didn't like other men ogling his chick. Chyna's body was for his eyes and his eyes only. She was testing his sanity by rockin' something so sexy and revealing but he played it cool. Tyreik eased her chair up to the table and sat opposite her.

"You look nice." He placed his elbow on the table and placed his hand up to his mouth.

Every part of him wanted to snatch her ass up for wearing such a daring outfit.

"Thank you." Chyna placed her napkin on her lap unfazed by his compliment.

She knew she looked good. His compliment wasn't confirmation of that. It wasn't until after their food was served that they began to discuss their situation. Chyna ate her Saltado de Langostinos and listened closely as Tyreik spoke.

"I'ma keep it real wit' you." He leaned forward.

"What were you doing, keepin' it fake wit' me before?" Chyna quizzed looking up from her plate.

Tyreik stopped chewing and mean mugged her. He wasn't in the mood for her smart mouth.

"I was talkin' to Rema," he confessed.

Chyna threw her fork down angrily and folded her arms across her chest.

"Thanks for ruining my fuckin' meal," she hissed. "If that's what you wanted to tell me, you could've told me that shit over the phone."

"Will you calm down? You blowin' shit way outta proportion. It was strictly on some cool shit. We was just checkin' up on each other. Nothing more, nothing less."

Chyna shot daggers at him with her eyes. She wanted to pick up her knife and stab him in the face with it. But she'd go to jail for that. Instead, she cleared her throat and rose to her feet.

"Where you going?" Tyreik questioned unsure of what she might do.

"I'm going to the bathroom." She grabbed her clutch.

She had to get away from him before she did something she might regret. Chyna had no idea what kind of power she had over the entire restaurant as she glided across the room but Tyreik did. He sat with his fist balled, infuriated. He hated how the other men in the restaurant watched as her round hips swayed. They were all practically salivating.

Tyreik knew she was going to the restroom on purpose. She was doing it to piss him off. It was working. Chyna was good at throwing subliminal shots. She wanted him to see that she was desirable too. He wasn't the only man that wanted her. Tyreik already knew that. That's why he didn't want anyone else to have her. He knew what a prize she was.

After taking a moment to gather her emotions, Chyna inhaled deep and exited the restroom. On the way back to the table every man stared at her with lustful eyes. One man in specifically couldn't take his eyes off of her. His name was Carlos. People on the streets called him Los. He sat at a table with a group of business associates. He should've been focusing on the conversation but Chyna had caught his attention and wouldn't let it go.

She was the most beautiful woman he'd ever seen. He'd never seen anything like her before. She was almost angelic and thick in all the right places. The curves of her hips swayed to their own beat. When she sauntered across the room it was as if she was walking on a cloud. He knew she was there with someone else but Carlos could tell that her man wasn't treating her right. There was sadness in her eyes that hid quietly beneath her blatant sex appeal.

He found himself wanting to hold her in his arms and calm her fears. But Chyna hadn't even noticed him. The dude she was with had her full attention. That didn't stop Carlos from wanting her. He had to take her from her man; that was his mission.

Feeling herself, Chyna swung her hair over her shoulder and did her best impression of a supermodel walking the catwalk. Tyreik hadn't taken his eyes off her for a second. Homeboy was heated. Chyna could see jealous rage in his eyes. Her plan was working. Holding her stomach in, she channeled Joan Smalls as she sashayed.

Chyna had it going on. She was doing good until her heel buckled and she almost fell. Her entire life flashed before eyes as she tried to stop herself from falling. *Elizabeth, I'm coming*, she thought as she almost hit the floor. Thankfully, her body never even got the chance to meet the ground. A man grabbed her before she ate it.

"Oh my God," she panicked leaning into the unknown man's arms.

"You good?" Carlos asked.

Chyna looked up into his warm eyes. Her heart instantly smiled.

"Yeah." She stood up straight and fixed herself.

"You sure?" He placed his hand on her arm.

"Yeah, I'm good. Thank you." Chyna flashed him a quick smile then walked off.

"You're welcome." Carlos replied wishing the moment would've lasted longer.

"What the fuck was that about?" Tyreik barked as soon as she sat down.

"Didn't you see me almost fall? He helped me up," she quipped.

"That's what you get for wearing that li'l bitty-ass dress. You ain't have to let him touch all on you like that."

"You can stop. He barely touched me. Now back to this bullshit you was tryin' to feed me. When I talked to Rema she made it seem like y'all was fuckin' around."

"Or is that how you took it? You know how you are. You take one thing and run wit' it. She simply said, 'ask him'; that's it. How you get we fuckin' around outta that?" He declared taking a sip of his drink.

Chyna bit her inner lip. Tyreik had a point. Maybe she had jumped the gun but nah… Chyna knew the game. Something was going on between him and Rema.

"Ok, if ain't nothin' going on then call her," she challenged.

"What? No, I'm not doing that." Tyreik shook his head.

"Why not? You tellin' the truth, right? Ain't shit going on. Y'all just friends so call and verify it." Chyna placed her shoulders back.

"What is that gonna prove? That you're crazy. I ain't even tryin' to play you like that," Tyreik said with a laugh. "You too pretty."

"First off, thank you; I am pretty." Chyna flung her hair to the side. "Second, I'm not crazy. Get yo' life. Third, fuck all that shit you talkin'. Call her."

"I ain't got her number no more. I erased it out my phone." Tyreik slouched down in his seat.

"Lies! Let me see. Prove it." Chyna held out her hand.

Tyreik gladly handed her his phone. Chyna scrolled through his contacts and Rema's number was nowhere to be found.

"I told her not to call me no more," Tyreik added.

Chyna rolled her eyes and handed him back his phone. It was apparent he wasn't going to call her. Chyna didn't even need him to call her. She already knew what it was; or did she? Tyreik was telling the truth. *No, don't be no fool, Chyna,* she told herself. She felt like she was going insane. She didn't know who or what to believe anymore.

Which should she ride with: her heart or her mind? Going with her heart always got her in trouble. Sitting across from Tyreik under the soft, amber flow of the candlelight, all Chyna wanted to do was leap in his arms. Being away from him the past few days had been torture. She loathed having to be cold-hearted towards him. Being soft and pink was who she was at the core of her.

"Tyreik, what the hell are we really doing?" Chyna sat back in her seat and pushed her plate away.

She'd become fed up all over again.

"We been together for fifteen years. We don't have any kids together. I mean, I know you care for India but y'all ain't really that close. I want y'all to have a better relationship. You're the only man she's ever been around except my brother and my dad."

"I love India. India just don't like to listen sometimes." He affirmed.

"That's because she don't respect you. She sees how you treat me."

"But it ain't just me though. You be turnin' up too." Tyreik pointed out.

"You're right," Chyna agreed. "We gotta stop arguing in front of her. I don't want her constantly seeing me sad. I most definitely don't want her thinking that's how relationships are supposed to be 'cause it's not."

"We both gotta do better. You gotta stop spazzin' out on me tho. Learn how to talk to me. You can't just start barkin' on me from the jump. When you do that, I don't hear shit you sayin'."

"You're right." Chyna had no choice but to concur.

It was hard for her to remain calm when she talked to Tyreik though. It seemed like when she did talk to him like she had some sense, he took her words for granted.

"And I need you to be romantic. We don't do shit together no more. You kick it wit' yo' homeboys more than you do with me."

"What we doing now?" Tyreik said flabbergasted.

"We're only here cause yo' ass is in trouble," Chyna shot.

Tyreik held his head down and laughed.

"A'ight, I got you, baby. Anything else?" He eyed her seductively.

"And you need to be figuring out when you gon' propose to me," Chyna smiled.

"Here you go."

"I'm for real. You already took up all my good years. I ain't giving you no more. Either you gon' propose to me this year or we gon' call it quits," Chyna announced seriously.

"I'ma propose to you when I get good and ready." Tyreik stood his ground.

"No, you're going to propose to me this year or I'ma leave yo' ass for good. I'm not playin'. I'm serious. If I'ma go through all this shit, I might as well be your wife going through it. I am not going to spend another year of my life being just your damn girlfriend."

"You serious, huh?" Tyreik asked curiously.

"Yes, I am."

"A'ight. Message received." He threw up his hands, surrendering.

Chyna and Tyreik didn't even finish their main course before they were back at her place making love. Naked, she lie anticipating his stroke. Each plunge of his dick sent her to the moon and back. Tyreik's tongue slowly twirled around her neck as her hips did the dutty wine. Like two stars colliding, Chyna moaned softly. If she ever lost him her heart would stop beating. All of her strength would turn into weakness.

Her hands caressed his back as they gazed into each other's eyes. There was no way she could face tomorrow if he wasn't in her future. Wanting him and never getting him kept her on the path of destruction and she knew it. But she couldn't let failure win.

Tyreik stroked her slowly. He could feel himself about to cum. Chyna was wet as hell. The sounds of her sweet whimpers tortured him. She didn't know the effect she had on him. He was obsessed with her. He never wanted to see her with another man. And although he knew she deserved better, he wasn't willing to let her go.

When she questioned if he loved her for real it infuriated him. In his own sick way he actually loved her endlessly. The two of them not being together was never an option. He would never understand life if there was no them. He often questioned if he'd ever get it right and be who she wanted him to be. Tyreik didn't know if he had it in him to be his absolute best. He didn't have a blueprint on what a good man was supposed to be.

He went off what he saw around him. All of his pot'nahs lied and cheated. They stayed on some fuck shit and their girls put up with it. He didn't understand why Chyna couldn't play her position and do the same.

Tears danced in Chyna's eyes as he quickened his pace. She was disappointed with herself for allowing him back so easily. It was only a matter of time before he hurt her again. Everything about their relationship was wrong. They'd always end up here, feeding each other hopes and promises neither of them would be able to fulfill. The cycle would never end.

"I love you." He kissed her lips, rotating between the top and the bottom.

"I love you too." Chyna moaned as tears spilled out onto her cheeks.

"LOVE SO DEEP FOR MY NIGGA. I'LL NEVER LET HIM GO AND I SWEAR I'LL NEVER QUIT HIM."

-JAZMINE SULLIVAN, HOOD LOVE

CHAPTER 8

It was the first day of spring. Chyna had just wrapped writing her next book titled Material Girl 3: Secrets and Betrayals. Her Material Girl series had been a tremendous hit with her readers. She couldn't wait for them to read the final installment to the series. Although there was some trepidation because with all the drama surrounding Tyreik and her relationship, she hadn't been able to really focus on the book like she wanted.

The book was good but it wasn't Chyna Black great. Chyna hated putting out work that she wasn't 100% proud of but her deadline was up. It didn't help that Tyreik never made good on his promise to buy her new laptop. She ended up having to purchase a new one herself. Needing to take her mind off her woes, Chyna and India headed over to her mother's house for Sunday dinner.

Tyreik stayed behind at their home. He wasn't welcome at her mother's house. Diane Peoples, Chyna's mom, couldn't stand him. Ever since he cheated on her and left her for Rema when she was younger, her mother didn't have an ounce of compassion for him. Like her friends, Diane felt Chyna could do much better than Tyreik.

In Diane's eyes, Tyreik did nothing but bring her down. Although Chyna never came to her mother with her problems anymore, India often told her grandmother about the stuff going on at home. Diane hated that her grandbaby was being subjected to such madness but she trusted that Chyna would come to her senses.

Everybody was at Diane's house. Chyna's brother, her Aunt Lauren and twin uncles Cory and Tory were there, including some of her little cousins. Chyna's childhood home was filled with the aroma of soul food. Her mother had outdone herself. She prepared homemade macaroni and cheese, greens, dressing, ham, fried chicken, a roast and dinner rolls. For dessert was strawberry shortcake. Chyna couldn't wait to dig in.

Everyone sat around the dinner table eating, laughing and catching up. Chyna savored her mother's dressing. She'd almost devoured it all. Outside of her daughter and her man, Chyna loved her mother dearly.

Diane was tough and outspoken but underneath her hard exterior was a loving, caring woman who loved her children more than life itself. Growing up, Diane hadn't been the picture perfect mother Chyna hoped for. Now that she was a parent herself, Chyna realized how easy it was to fuck up as a mom. She tried to do the best she could but no one was perfect.

It didn't dawn on Chyna when she was young, but her mother was learning as she went along. It was the same for Chyna now. At the dinner table Chyna looked over at her mama and her heart smiled. Diane was getting prettier with age. She was about to turn 55 that June.

She no longer worked as a bank teller. She was the proud owner of a daycare. She had a beautiful home that she'd lived in for 21 years. Diane was no longer the hot girl she was when Chyna was a kid. She barely left the house unless she was heading to the grocery story, Wal-Mart, Home Depot or Target. She didn't have many friends. For fun, she gambled online and decorated her house.

One of Chyna's biggest fears in life was ending up like her. None of the women in her family were married. They were all single mothers and alone. Chyna dreaded being in her fifties and not having anyone in her life to share it with.

She felt sorry for her mother. She'd pushed everyone in her life away except her kids. Now that she was getting older in age, she clung to them for dear life.

Chyna wanted to break the cycle and prove that a Peoples woman was lovable enough to be someone's wife.

"Chyna, when is your next book coming out?" Her Uncle Tory asked.

"In June." She drank her grape, Vess soda.

"How many you got out now?" One of her cousins chimed in.

"I have no idea. Too many to count." She answered relishing the food.

"You know one of my coworkers is tryin' to write a book of poetry. I told her you wrote books so she asked if you could call her and help her. She wants to know how to publish it." Cory picked his teeth with his straw.

"I don't know anything about poetry." Chyna continued to eat her food.

She didn't understand why people thought she would want to talk to perfect strangers about publishing their books. Chyna didn't mind helping people out but she had to draw a line somewhere.

"You gon' be in Hollywood soon, girl. When they gon' turn one of yo' books into a movie?" Lauren said energetically.

Chyna stopped chewing and paused before responding. If she spoke before thinking she would've probably replied, "Who are 'they'?" She knew her family and the fifty million other people that asked her that question meant well but the question made absolutely no sense. It cracked her up and irritated her that people thought it was that easy for a book to be turned into a movie.

Like at the snap of her fingers she had the clout to make it happen. The industry was fickle and shady as hell. Yes, Chyna was a successful author but she didn't have Hollywood connections. She wished she did but she didn't. Her family and people on social media just assumed that Hollywood was beating down her door. Chyna wanted nothing more than to break into television and movies but stuff like that took time. She didn't have a foot in the door yet but through hard work and determination she would get there.

"Somebody has to offer me a deal first." She swallowed her food. "Mama, did you put me a plate up so I can take some food home?" She changed the subject.

"I put you and India up a plate," Diane said sternly.

She was not here to feed Chyna, India and her boyfriend. As far as she was concerned, the nigga could starve.

"Mama, didn't nobody ask you to fix Tyreik a plate." Chyna groaned not in the mood for a lecture.

"Where your man at, girl, anyway? Why he ain't here?" Lauren asked being nosey.

"'Cause he wasn't invited." Diane responded before Chyna could.

"Why not? You don't like him, Die?"

"No… I …. Do... Not. I can't stand the li'l ugly boy. He look like a big ole gorilla," Diane snarled. "I don't know why she like him. He makes my stomach hurt every time I see him. The man has a fetus face."

"Let me find out you a hater, Mama." Chyna laughed her mother's remarks off.

She didn't like it when her mother talked about Tyreik but she was used to it now. Chyna learned over the years to keep her head down and her mouth shut. There was no point in arguing with Diane. Chyna would lose every time.

"No, you a fool for dealing wit' his trifling-ass. India be telling me how y'all be over there cussing and fighting at each other all the time."

Chyna cut her eyes at her daughter. She'd told her numerous times to keep what happened at home between them. India knew better than to tell her business. India looked like a dear caught in headlights.

"Miss Diane," she shrilled.

India didn't call Diane grandma or granny. When she was a toddler attending her grandma's daycare, she heard the other kids call her Diane so she started to call her that as well.

"I told you not to say nothin'!" India whined.

"First of all, stay in a child's place." Diane checked her. "You don't tell me nothin'. And I just had to say something."

"Ok, you said something. Now let it go," Chyna said embarrassed.

She didn't want her whole family knowing her business. It was bad enough that she looked like a fool in her mother's eyes. She didn't want to be viewed the same by her family. Diane knew she had taken things too far and hushed. She didn't get to spend that much time with her daughter and didn't want to spend the time she had with her arguing.

"I'm sorry. I just don't like to hear that y'all be arguing all the time."

"What couple doesn't argue," Chyna countered. "Yes, we have our problems but Tyreik and I love each other. He's a good man. I wouldn't be with him if he wasn't. He loves me and India. We've even been talkin' about getting married." Chyna threw in for good measure.

"He's been ring shopping and everything." She lied but she had to save face.

She had to prove her mother wrong. She had to convince them all that she had everything under control.

After being ridiculed at dinner by her mother, Chyna couldn't wait to get home. It was the one time in her life she hated not knowing how to drive. If she did know how, she would've been left. Unfortunately, she had to wait until someone was ready to leave so she could hitch a ride with them. Mentally exhausted, she slowly made her way up the staircase leading to her room.

To her surprise, when she rounded the corner she saw tea candles lining the steps. A smile instantly spread on her face. She didn't know what Tyreik was up to but she was down to find out. Chyna took each step one-by-one anticipating the surprise which awaited her. The heart throbbing, sweet, sensual sound of SiR's *Perfect Remedy* serenaded her ears as she made her way to the top of the stairs.

Her hardwood floors were covered with pink rose petals. Standing in the midst of the beautiful array of love stood Tyreik. He was completely shirtless. He only wore a pair of jeans that hung low off his hips showcasing the Ken Doll slits in his pelvis. His strong pecks, biceps and abs twinkled under the candlelight. He resembled an African god. Chyna thanked God that he was hers.

"Hi, pretty girl." He spoke in a low, raspy tone.

"What is all of this?" She beamed with joy.

"I know you've been stressed out about your book and everything else so I wanted to do something that would put a smile on your face." He handed her a glass of champagne.

"Aww, babe, this is so sweet." She stood on her tip toes and gave him a big kiss. "You didn't have to do this." She said almost on the verge of tears.

"You said you wanted me to be more romantic. Plus, you deserve it." He took her hand and led her to the master bathroom.

Inside the bathroom were even more flowers and candles. A bubble bath filled with rose petals, a bottle of champagne and chocolate covered strawberries awaited her.

"Take off your clothes." Tyreik instructed with his arms wrapped around her tiny waist.

Melting from his touch, Chyna did exactly as she was told. Piece by piece she slipped out of her clothes. When she was done she headed over to the tub where Tyreik awaited her. He was already inside. Chyna eased her way into the steaming hot water and rested her back on his muscular chest. Her head rested against his neck. For the first time in weeks, she was able to exhale. With her eyes closed she said a silent prayer to God thanking him for the moment and Tyreik.

"How was dinner?" He asked taking a sponge and sensually washing her body.

"It was cool until my mama started talkin' shit about you," Chyna remarked.

"Your ole bird stay talkin' shit about me. What's new?" He chuckled unbothered.

"Right. Then I found out India has been talkin' to her about us which I didn't like. I was just ready to come home after that."

"I understand. India gon' have to learn how to stay out of grown folks business tho." Tyreik made her raise her arm so he could wash her armpit. "You a li'l ripe under there," he teased.

"Shut up." Chyna playfully hit him.

"Ok, give me your top five favorite MC's?" He asked wanting to take her mind off of dinner.

Chyna's long hair clung to the nape of her neck. She couldn't contain her smile. Top Five was a game she and Tyreik often played. They were both avid music lovers and sports fans. Their list for each topic varied greatly.

"Right now or of all time?"

"Of all time." He massaged her shoulders.

"Oh my God that feels so good." Chyna closed her eyes and delighted in his touch.

"C'mon; top five."

"Ok-ok." Chyna came back to the present. "Top five MC's of all time," she thought. "Tupac, Jay-Z, Kendrick Lamar...Nas and Biggie.

"You trippin'," Tyreik smirked. "Mine are Biggie, Nas, Jigga, Slick Rick the Ruler, K. Dot and Rakim."

"Slick Rick, really?" She gazed at him over her shoulder. "Oh, I forgot you were born in the 70's," Chyna gagged. "And nigga, that was six."

"That's real hip hop for yo' ass."

"If you say so," she replied mockingly. "Hell, you might as well have said the Sugar Hill Gang." Chyna doubled over in laughter.

"You done?" Tyreik glared at her unwilling to laugh.

"Ok…" Chyna gained her composure. "Name your top five favorite female singers of all time."

"I don't listen to too many females but I guess I would have to say Erykah Badu…Jill Scott, Babygirl AKA Aaliyah… uhhhhh—"

"All I know is Beyoncé better be on that list." Chyna cautioned.

She would make that nigga pack his bags in get out if she wasn't.

"Beyoncé," Tyreik grinned. "Annnnnnd…," He thought for a second. "Celine Dion."

"Celine Dion?" Chyna whipped her head around so hard her wet hair smacked him in the face. "Where the hell that come from? Let me find out you got something you need to tell me."

She joked about him being gay.

"Don't get punched in the throat," he warned. "Celine Dion be singing about some real shit. That Titanic song was the business."

"Boooooooooooo!" Chyna gave him a thumbs a down. "Your top five sucked. My top five are queen muva Beyoncé of course, the vocal bible herself Brandy, the former blonde bombshell Faith Evans, will sing you under the table Jazmine Sullivan and the legendary Miss Anita Baker."

"Ok," Tyreik laughed. "You got that off."

"I sure did." Chyna snapped her finger.

These were the moments that made her fall in love with him. These were the moments that made her never want to leave his side. Tyreik could be a handful most of the time but he was also sweet and thoughtful.

He knew how to please her and keep her satisfied. He was her best friend. She wished her family and friends could see him when he was like this. He wasn't always an ass. There was a softer side to him that only she was blessed to see. Tyreik held her close. He could feel the tension in her body slowly being released. Nothing pleased him more than making Chyna happy.

He did so much shit that disappointed her that times like this were a rarity. All he wanted to do was make her feel complete when she was next to him. If she was good then so was he. He didn't give a fuck about what the naysayers had to say. They didn't know his heart or his intentions. No other woman would ever come before Chyna. He was put on earth to love her. Nothing or no one was going to tear them apart.

"I'VE BEEN BLEEDING IN YOUR SILENCE."

-CHRIS BROWN FEAT. KENDRICK LAMAR, AUTUMN LEAVES

CHAPTER 9

A few months had gone by. Chyna found herself in a really good space. Everything in her life was pretty much back to normal. She and Tyreik hadn't had any hiccups since Phone Gate. He'd been on his P's and Q's. Chyna could finally breathe and focus on the other important things in her life, one of them being her book. Her first set of edits were back and she only had a week to review them and make any necessary changes.

Chyna only had a few days left and she still had so much more work that needed to be done. Her neck and back were killing her. She was tired as hell but none of that mattered. Her book was her main priority. She had her night light on, her music playing and a cold bottle of water by her side.

She was ready to pull an all nighter. Thankfully, Chyna's room was her sanctuary. She had a huge, loft-style bedroom. It was so big that each section of the room had its purpose. One wing was her office.

She had a desktop computer, fax machine/printer, file cabinet, roll-away chair and vision board. In the center of the room was her king size bed and entertainment system that housed her flatscreen TV, DVD player, DVR and movies. Next to her bedding area was her makeup/filming vicinity. Chyna did her makeup and filmed her All Tea, All Shade videos at her IKEA *Micke* desk. Behind her when she filmed was a black and white wall with a wall of gold mirrors and a black bench.

The clock on her computer read 3:10a.m. India was in her room sound asleep. Like always, Tyreik was out in the streets. He'd been gone since earlier that afternoon. That night he was throwing a party at Lola with Kingston. They'd brought Solange in town to DJ. Chyna wished she was there to witness the turn up but nothing came before her career.

She was sure that chicks were all on Tyreik but she couldn't worry about that. She couldn't constantly run in behind him to make sure he behaved. If he was up to no good, whatever was in the dark, would eventually come to light. Chyna was in the midst of reading over chapter 14 when her phone rang. A smile spread across her face. It was Tyreik.

"Hello?" She sang.

"Hey, babe."

"Hi." She spoke back.

Chyna couldn't help but hear the chatter in the background.

"Where you at?" She turned up her face.

"I'm at Uncle Bill's 'bout to grab something to eat. You want me to bring you something back?" Tyreik spoke louder than necessary.

It quickly became obvious that he was drunk. Chyna hated when he got lit. In the beginning of his intoxicated stage he was always cool but when he passed the line of being tipsy, he became angry and destructive. Chyna didn't feel like babysitting his drunk-ass that night.

"No. Who you at Uncle Bill's wit'?"

"I'm with the same people I told you I was wit' before. It's a whole gang of us."

"So you wit' Kingston?" She questioned.

"And my pot'nah Rob."

"Oh really, so this Rob person really does exist?" Chyna's voice dripped with sarcasm.

"Yeah, he does. You wanna talk to him?"

"Yep, put him on the phone."

"Hold on. Ay yo, Rob. My lady wanna holla at you for a second." Tyreik handed him the phone.

"Hello?" Rob said in a deep tone.

"Hi, how you doing?"

"I'm good," he chuckled.

"I just wanted to make sure you were real," Chyna giggled.

"I'm real, baby girl."

"Alright. You can put Tyreik back on the phone."

"A'ight, hold on." Rob tossed Tyreik his cell.

"She crazy, dawg. Don't mind her," Tyreik joked. "You good now, baby?'

"Yeah, just hurry up and get home."

"Oh, I got something to tell you too." Tyreik lowered his tone.

"What?" Chyna immediately went on guard.

"I copped some new Giovanna Rims for the whip today," he gushed.

"You did what?" Chyna scowled.

He hadn't helped her with the rent in months but had the nerve to go buy a new set of rims.

"You taking that shit back tomor," she snapped.

"You out your muthafuckin' mind. My rims ain't going nowhere," Tyreik laughed her off.

"Tyreik! I thought you was gon' give me some of your eggs." A chick said in the background.

"Who the hell is that?" Chyna sat straight up in her chair.

The girl who called his name said it way too sweet. Chyna could hear in her voice that she was trying to get the D. She didn't have the time nor the energy to be catching a case.

"Calm down, baby. That's one of the homegirls. Don't trip."

"Homegirl my ass. If I ain't never met the bitch, then she ain't none of yo' damn friend. And you know I don't do that friend shit no way! Friends fuck friends!" She spat. "It's some hoes wit' y'all? On my mama, don't make me come up there 'cause you know I will."

"How you gon' get here? In a cab?" Tyreik laughed hysterically.

"Try me." Chyna rolled her neck.

"A'ight, li'l crazy-ass girl. Let me finish eating and I'll be home in a minute." Tyreik tried to get off the phone.

"Tyreik, don't you hang up this phone! I'm not done talkin' to you!"

"I'll see you in a minute, babe." He hung up anyway.

"Tyreik!" Chyna called out his name to no avail.

She didn't like it one bit that Tyreik was around a bunch of girls. Kingston was always trying to have him on a ho mission. If the tables were turned and she were out in the wee hours of the morning with a bunch of niggas, he'd lose his damn mind. He would've broken up with her right then and there. Chyna tried taking her mind off of Tyreik and his early morning escapades, but an hour later when he still wasn't home, she became paranoid. Chyna picked up her phone and texted him.

<Messages   **Tyreik**   Details

U should be done eatin' by now!

Chyna sent the text and waited for his reply. While she waited, she started working back on her book. She was so into what she was doing that she didn't' even notice a half an hour had gone by with no response.

"Oh hell nah. He ain't responded." She hissed calling his phone.

To Chyna's dismay the phone rang and rang until his voicemail clicked in. Taken aback that he didn't answer the phone, she called again. Once more the phone rang and she got no answer. Chyna held her phone in her hand and stared absently at the computer screen.

Her whole entire body had gone numb. She could feel that Tyreik was on some BS in her veins. *Chill out, Chyna,* she ran her fingers though her hair. *Maybe he's on his way home and has the music turned up,* she told herself. *Yeah, that's it. He'll be home in a minute. You have nothin' to worry about.*

By 7am Chyna was losing her shit. She'd called Tyreik damn near fifty times. Back-to-back she called. After a while it stopped ringing and she was forwarded to voicemail. She really lost it then. *I'ma kill him,* she promised herself. He had to be with another chick. She swore the next time Tyreik pulled one of his infamous stunts he was out the door but she had no proof he was with another girl.

All she had was the gut wrenching suspicion inside her stomach. *Maybe he got locked up.* The nigga was riding around with a suspended license and expired plates. That had to have been the reason he hadn't made it home and wasn't answering the phone. Worried sick, Chyna located Kingston's number and hit him up. She hated involving other people in their mess but in a situation like this, she had no other choice. Chyna walked in circles around her bedroom as the phone rang.

"Hello?" Kingston answered groggily.

Chyna felt bad for waking him up out of his sleep.

"Hey, Kingston. My bad for callin' so late but I'm lookin' for Tyreik. Is he wit' you?" She asked on pins and needles.

"Nah, I ain't seen that nigga since we left the club." He replied half asleep.

Kingston had no idea that he was incriminating his friend. Normally, he would've had a lie prepared.

"Ok, thanks." Chyna sucked her teeth before throwing her phone down on the bed.

"This nigga lied to me again." She said out loud on the verge of having an aneurism.

When Tyreik got her this upset her blood pressure skyrocketed. The only thing she could concentrate on was her rage. Only Tyreik had this kind of effect on her. She never even knew a person could experience that type of fury.

It was the non-stop lies and disrespect that infuriated her the most. Just as Chyna was about to call his phone and leave him a scathing voicemail message, she heard the front door open. A sense of relief swept over her body. She was happy that he wasn't locked up or hurt. That didn't take away that he'd lied to her and stayed out all night. Plus, she was mad that he'd spent his money from the party on a set of new rims.

Tyreik drunkenly made his way up the steps. He knew he was in for a verbal tongue lashing. He'd prepared himself for it. As soon as his hazy eyes rested on Chyna he couldn't help but grab his crotch and laugh. The fact that he had the nerve to laugh at her pissed her off even more.

"What the fuck is so funny? I've been callin' you for the past three hours."

"My phone died," he hiccuped.

"I thought yo' dumb-ass was dead or in jail."

"My bad, babe." Tyreik stumbled backwards almost falling down the steps. "Whoa." He caught himself.

"That's what yo' stupid-ass get," Chyna spat.

Grinning from ear to ear, Tyreik walked over and wrapped her up in his arms. He reeked of liquor. Chyna could even smell the faint hint of another woman's perfume.

"You mad at me?" Tyreik kissed her neck sloppily.

"What you think?" She pushed him off of her. "You stink."

"That's fucked up." Tyreik licked his bottom lip and shot her a sexy glance.

Chyna's clit automatically jumped. *Focus, bitch.*

"Where you been this whole time?" She placed her hands on her hips.

"We went on the Eastside." Tyreik explained, kicking off his shoes.

"Who is we?" Chyna eyed him closely.

"Me and Kingston." Tyreik pulled his shirt off over his head.

His broad chest called her name. She wanted to run her tongue across each one of his tattoos.

"You's a black-ass lie!"Chyna swung her arm in the air. "I called Kingston lookin' for you and he said he hadn't seen you since y'all left the club."

"Damn, my bad. Did I say Kingston? You're right; he wasn't with us. I meant Kay." He replied with a straight face.

"You know what? Yo' ass should've been a detective instead of an author. 'Cause you be searching for all the clues." He chuckled falling back onto the bed.

"Why the hell you lie to me?" Chyna shook his arm to keep him awake.

"What I lie to you about?" Tyreik mumbled damn near asleep.

"About being wit' Kingston. Y'all was wit' some hoes, weren't you?"

"I don't know what you talkin' about," Tyreik replied before passing out.

"Tyreik!" Chyna tried to wake him up. "Tyreik!"

There was no waking him up. He was knocked out. Not satisfied with the bullshit-ass answers he'd given her, she channeled her anger towards revenge. If he thought he was going to stay out all times of the night, lie about who he was with and buy new rims while she paid all the bills, he had another thing coming. He should've known Chyna wasn't going to let that ride.

Tyreik lie on his back snoring loudly, oblivious to what was going on around him. The sight of him disgusted

Chyna. She had to do something to make herself feel better. While he slept like a drunk, overgrown baby, she ran his pockets. He had $1,500 left. Chyna took $300 off the top then went into the bathroom and grabbed his toothbrush. Without hesitation, she lifted the toilet seat and ran his toothbrush along the inner rim of the toilet.

You wanna kick it with other hoes? Let's see how them hoes like yo' shitty-ass breath, she thought with a sly grin on her face. Pleased with her results, she placed the toothbrush back in the holder and moved hers to the medicine cabinet. Still not fulfilled, Chyna skipped down the steps to the kitchen. She pulled open the cutlery drawer and picked up a dinner knife.

A sadistic smile was etched on her lips as she walked outside. The morning sun greeted her as she located Tyreik's truck. The new black rims shined in the morning light. In order for Tyreik to get the new rims he had to get a set of new tires so the rims would fit.

Chyna looked around to make sure the coast was clear. It was. Swiftly, she bent down and rammed the knife into his back right tire. If Tyreik was going to fuck her over, she was going to fuck him over ten times harder. There was always a price to pay when you played dirty.

Tyreik staying out all night and disrespecting her would surely cost him in more ways than one.

"IN THIS VERY MOMENT I'M KING."

-NICKI MINAJ, MOMENT FOR LIFE

CHAPTER 10

After only a few hours of sleep, Chyna was back up and at it. She'd lost valuable work time dealing with Tyreik and his latest shenanigans. Tyreik lie in bed still asleep. He was still partially clothed. Chyna didn't even bother to help him out of his jeans. As far as she was concerned, he could fend for himself.

"Mom!" India called her name from the other side of the door.

India knew not to just walk in her mother's room without permission. Chyna never wanted her daughter to catch her in a compromising position again. When India was around 7 she was outside playing with the neighborhood kids; Chyna and Tyreik were in the house during the middle of the day getting freaky.

Tyreik lie on his back fully naked while Chyna sat between his legs on her knees giving him head. They were so into the act that when India ran into the house and tried to bust through the door, Chyna nearly jumped out of her skin. Thankfully, she had the chain on the door so India only saw her mother's ass up in the air and Tyreik's bare legs. After that debacle, Chyna made sure that India knew to knock first.

"Yeah, babe," she answered.

"I'm hungry. Can I fix me something to eat?"

"I don't care."

"Do we have anything healthy?"

"What?" Chyna grinned.

"I've decided that I'm going to eat better. No more bad foods for me. I'm even thinking about going vegan, so are there any healthy snacks?"

"Yeah, you can eat tissue. It tastes like clouds," Chyna responded sarcastically.

"Mooooom!" India cackled. "Stop playing!"

"No, we don't have any healthy snacks. When Tyreik get up I'll have him take me to the grocery store. I need to get some food anyway."

"Ok." India ran back to her room.

Tyreik stirred in his sleep and opened his eyes. Homeboy was a threw piece. He'd got lit the night before. The turn up for him and his crew was real. Tyreik lived his life like a movie. He was the modern day Jay Gatsby.

Everyday was a party for him. Clubbing, poppin' bottles, being fly, blowing cash and stuntin' on niggas was a high for him.

He loved the attention he got from the streets. Young cats revered him. They wanted to live the rock star lifestyle he led not knowing that Tyreik barely had two nickels to rub together. Appearances were everything and Tyreik was good at putting on a show. He wanted more out of life. He just didn't know how to get there.

He was used to moving kilos from state to state. Being a party promoter with Kingston was cool. It gave him the clout he wanted and the local recognition he craved. It kept his name alive in the streets. Tyreik needed the notoriety and the street fame. He was used to being a trap star but now Chyna was better known than he was.

He'd basically schooled her on the game and made her the woman she was. She'd taken their relationship hardships and turned it into a best-selling novel. Now she was winning. She ruled the world. Tyreik low-key hated going places with her. He was jealous of all the attention she got. Chyna was known all over the world.

She'd sold just as many books as he sold dope during his run. He was happy that she'd found her niche in the world and was living her dream. Chyna would often go to Tyreik for advice on her books. He happily obliged 'cause he wanted to see his baby win but a part of him couldn't help but resent her.

When she was younger, Chyna clung to him for dear life. She needed him in every way imaginable. Back in the day, financially, she couldn't make a move without him. Now if she woke up one day and decided she didn't want to be with him anymore, she could end things without hesitation. Tyreik knew deep in his heart that the only thing keeping her around at this point was her love for him.

Being where she was at in her career, she deserved someone on her level. Tyreik could never be what she wanted. He would never fit into her world. He didn't know anything about hard work. Everything in life for him was easy. If it was too complicated or challenging, he didn't want to have anything to do with it. Chyna on the other hand fought and scrapped for every success she ever had. She wasn't afraid to crawl through the mud in order to get to glory.

Yet he couldn't imagine life without her. She was his better half, his rib, his reason for living. Tyreik revered her and disliked her at the same time. He knew it was just a matter of time before the plans God had for her would eclipse the feelings she had for him. Reeling from his hangover, Tyreik rolled out of bed. His feet rested on the floor as he rubbed the cold out of his eyes.

"Man." He groaned arching his back.

"You finally got yo' ass up, I see." Chyna wasted no time starting in on him.

"What time is it?"

"A little after three." She continued to type on the computer.

"Damn, it don't even seem like I slept that long." He rose from the bed and walked over to her. "You mad at me?" He asked hugging her from behind.

"Ugh... get away from me. Your breath stink." Chyna rolled her shoulder to make him move.

"Don't act like you don't love me and my stankin' ass breath." Tyreik kissed her cheek.

"Eww… go brush your teeth," Chyna shrilled.

"Shut up. Quit actin' like a girl." Tyreik playfully mushed her in the back of her head.

"I'ma beat yo' ass!" Chyna turned to hit him but missed.

Tyreik went into the bathroom. He took a long piss then turned on the faucet. After washing his hands, he grabbed his toothbrush. Chyna went and stood in the doorway of the bathroom. She watched with glee as he placed toothpaste on the bristles then placed it in his mouth. An array of rainbows and butterflies danced in her chest. Nothing was better than revenge served cold, especially when the person didn't even see it coming.

"You gon' explain to me why you lied to me again?" She cocked her head to the side.

Tyreik proceeded to brush his tongue without responding. Chyna knew he was thinking of a lie. As he did, all she could imagine were shit particles swishing around in his mouth. Finished brushing his teeth, Tyreik rinsed his mouth out with water and mouthwash then looked at her through the mirror.

"I just woke up. Are you really about to start?" He asked already exasperated.

"You started with me when you decided to walk yo' black ass up in here at 7:00 in the damn morning, like it was all good."

"Don't you gotta book to write?" He bypassed her not in the mood.

His head was spinning and he could barely stand up straight.

"Don't worry about my book. I got this. You need to answer the damn question." Chyna spun around and faced him. "You lied and said you were with Kingston and Kingston's ass was at home the whole time asleep. And what you go on the Eastside for? Ain't nothin' on the Eastside but strippers and trouble."

"That's why I went... for the strippers," Tyreik joked.

"Akikikiki," Chyna pretended to laugh then rolled her eyes. "Yo' ass got jokes I see. And who told you to go buy some expensive-ass rims? You could'a put that money on a bill, bruh!"

"Who said I wasn't gon' help you?" He reached in his pocket and pulled out three bills. "I ain't got that much but here."

He handed her $140. He had no idea that she knew how much money he really had. Chyna looked at the money and blinked. *Did this nigga really just give me a $140? He ain't paid not nall bill in this muthafucka in months and this all I get? This muthafucka stingy as hell. That's why I don't feel bad about robbin' his ass. Just for that, I'ma poke a hole in all of his damn tires.* Chyna wanted so bad to go off but she couldn't blow her cover and let him know she'd went through his pockets.

"What?" He looked at her.

He could see the displeasure on her face.

"Nothin'." She placed the money in her bra along with the rest of the money she'd stolen hours before. "Thank you. Now why weren't you answering your phone?" She continued her line of questioning. "You forwarded me to voicemail."

"'Cause I ain't wanna hear your fuckin' mouth. I knew you were gon' feel some type of way so I figured I'd deal with you when I got home."

"Oh, so now you have to deal with me? I'ma burden to you?" Chyna squinted her eyes.

"You're ridiculous," Tyreik smirked. "I gotta get some food in my system. I don't feel good." He rubbed his stomach.

"That's what yo' ass get. I need you to take me to the grocery store anyway."

"Bet, let's go. I'll fry some chicken or something," Tyreik volunteered.

Chyna and Tyreik made a quick run to Shop 'n Save but on the way back home his truck began to wobble and shake. His back, right tire started to go out on him.

"What the fuck?" He pulled over on the side of the road.

"It feel like you gotta flat." Chyna tried her hardest not to grin.

"I just got these tires yesterday. They fuckin' brand new." Tyreik cut off the engine.

"God don't like ugly." Chyna picked invisible lint off her shirt.

"Whatever," Tyreik fumed getting out of the car.

Chyna watched him examine the tire. He was pissed to say the least. Tyreik would not only have to place a doughnut on his truck but he'd have to ride around with it until the following day because it was a Sunday. He wouldn't be hitting the streets that night. Chyna had ruined his day just like he ruined her night.

"NEVER GET MAD AT SOMEONE FOR BEING WHO THEY'VE ALWAYS BEEN. BE UPSET WITH YOURSELF FOR NOT COMING TO TERMS WITH IT SOONER."- SOURCE UNKNOWN

CHAPTER 11

Wrapped up in Tyreik's arms, Chyna lie content. The May sun was peeking through the blinds as she smiled. She had a fabulous night getting her back cracked by him. He had her in every position known and unknown to man. Tyreik did her body right. She was sexually satisfied and at ease. It was Mother's Day. She was sure that Tyreik and her sexual escapades were a lead up to a fabulous day.

Naked, she rubbed his arm. The hair on his forearm soothed her fingertips. If time allowed it, she would lie there with him forever. She truly savored every moment she spent with him. When they weren't beefin', which was a rarity, it was all love between them. They were the best of friends.

She loved that she could talk to him about anything. Big or small, it didn't matter; he always made her feel her thoughts were important. She'd told Tyreik things that she never even uttered to her friends. She valued his opinion and how easily conversation flowed between them. Dying to hear the sound of his voice against her ear, she shook his arm.

"Leave me alone. I'm not ready to get up yet," he groaned.

"Get up and play with me." Chyna spoke in a baby voice.

"Oh, you ready for round four?" Tyreik poked her with his stiff dick.

"Uh ah, I can't take no more of that devil stick. I'm already going to be sore for the rest of the week. I ain't in my 20's no more. You can't be fuckin' me like that and expecting me to bounce back," she joked.

"You so wack," he teased.

"Nah, nigga, that after the club dick ain't no joke."

"Just call me King Ding-a-Ling." He leaped up and swung his dick from side-to-side causing it to slap against his thighs.

"Are you conscious?" Chyna looked up at him furrowing her brows.

"You know you want this dick." He fell on top of her and placed a sea of small kisses all over her face.

"I can't stand you." She wrapped her arms around his neck and took pleasure in each kiss.

"You love me?" He asked biting her neck.

"Yes!" She squealed in delight.

"You better." He slapped her thigh before getting up.

"You get on my nerves." Chyna sat up and rubbed her neck.

"You like it. Stop whining and come get in the shower with me." Tyreik held out his hand for her.

Chyna giddily obliged his request.

By the time Chyna was showered and dressed it began to register that Tyreik hadn't told her Happy Mother's Day once. Perplexed, she figured that by the time they went downstairs he would tell her and give her a gift. She was shocked when she entered her dining room. India was seated at the table. There were pink balloons everywhere.

On the center of the table was a vase filled with Peony flowers. Peonies were Chyna's favorite flower. The table was set with her best China and breakfast had already been prepared and placed on the table family-style. There were eggs, bacon, sausage, French toast, cantaloupe, strawberries and orange juice. Chyna was overwhelmed with joy. Tyreik had come through for her. He hadn't forgotten about her.

"Happy Mother's Day, Mom!" India yelled.

"Thank you, my baby." Chyna hugged her daughter tight and kissed her cheek.

Chyna's eyes welled with tears. She loved her family so much.

"Thank you, Tyreik. You outdid yourself, baby." She turned and hugged him.

"I ain't have nothing to do with this," he replied reluctantly. "This was all India."

Stunned, Chyna stepped back confused.

"Yeah, Mom, I did this all by myself," India stated proudly.

"Oh." Chyna replied coming to terms with the info she was given. "Well, thank you, babydoll. I can't believe you did all of this on your own. You are such a li'l woman now." She ruffled her hair and forced herself to smile.

"This shit look fire." Tyreik rubbed his hands eagerly. "India, you did that." He grabbed his plate.

He couldn't wait to dive in. Selfishly, Tyreik sat at the table and filled his plate. The nigga didn't even bother to say grace or tell Chyna Happy Mother's Day. The only thing he was concerned with was feeding his fat face. Feeling totally overlooked and taken for granted, Chyna sat at the table and pretended to be happy for India's sake. She would never let her daughter see the disappointment that lie behind her eyes after she'd gone above and beyond for her.

"India, you happy school about to let out soon?" Tyreik asked chewing on a piece of bacon.

"Yeah."

"You in the 10th grade, right?"

"No," India screwed up her face and stared at him like he was stupid. "I'm in 7th grade. You don't remember coming to the 7th grade science fair a few weeks ago?"

"Aww yeah, that was pretty cool," Tyreik nodded his head oblivious that he'd insulted her.

"So you not gon' tell me Happy Mother's Day?" Chyna blurted out of nowhere.

Tyreik looked at her.

"Oh my bad. Happy Mother's Day, babe." He leaned over and kissed her on the cheek then resumed eating.

This is some bullshit, she thought. *This nigga can't even remember me on Mother's Day.* Chyna felt bad that she couldn't fully enjoy her Mother's Day feast. It was eating away at her that Tyreik hadn't even acknowledged her. He acted as if it were another, regular day. This was the second holiday that year where she hadn't received a thing from him. The negro didn't even get her a card on Valentine's Day.

With all the shit she dealt with, he should've been waiting on her hand and foot. To her, it was a slap in the face. Hell, he still hadn't even proposed yet. Chyna was hanging on by a thread. At any moment, she was about to explode.

"I SEE THE PAIN, BABY, DEEP IN YOUR EYES, EVEN THOUGH YOU'RE SMILING."

-DAVE HOLLISTER, WE'VE COME TOO FAR

CHAPTER 12

A week had gone by and Chyna still hadn't gotten over Mother's Day Gate. Tyreik walked around as if nothing was wrong. He went on with life without a care in the world. The fact that he didn't see anything wrong with how he treated her, angered Chyna to the core. She went above and beyond for him.

She never missed a birthday or holiday. Chyna always put his needs before hers. Tyreik never went without. Over the last couple of years, she started to peep that the gifts had started to dry up. The only time he bought her anything was for Christmas. Every year for her birthday, Chyna threw herself a huge, extravagant party. For some reason, Tyreik always had an attitude and ruined it.

Sometimes she wondered if he was secretly jealous of her. Her friends sure did think so. They said they could see the jealousy in his eyes sometimes. Chyna quickly nixed the thought. Why would Tyreik be jealous of her? She was just regular ole Chyna. But Chyna had to think about it.

Outside of being good at selling drugs, throwing a party and dressing well, Tyreik wasn't successful at anything. He hadn't even traveled for real. Chyna often wondered what he was going to do with the rest of his life. Was the party ever going to stop? He damn well couldn't be in his 40's and 50's still going to the club every night.

He had to eventually settle down and grow some roots. Or then again, maybe this was who he was. Maybe Tyreik would always be a selfish, inconsiderate, lying prick. Chyna was starting to wonder were the good parts she loved about him worth fighting for anymore. The bad parts of him outweighed the good by pounds.

It was becoming harder and harder to carry around the burden he'd placed on her heart. Chyna was tired of going through the motions. She was sick of the instability. She never felt truly comfortable with him. He always kept her on her toes and not in a positive way. Her home was no longer a place of peace for her. It was filled with pain, anger and regret. Tension swarmed her.

It was as if a demonic spirit resided there. Chyna and Tyreik were always at odds. She couldn't go another year of her life living on a wish and a prayer. She'd reached the point of no return. Disgusted by the sight of his face, she tried her damnedest to keep her cool. Everything that had transpired over the last five months was wearing her down.

Tyreik sat opposite her in the sitting room. He smoked a fat blunt. It irritated her that he was blind to the fact that he was slowly driving her insane. Couldn't he see how unhappy she was? If he did, why didn't he care? Chyna didn't understand how someone could be so insensitive to how they treated other people. Chyna didn't know if she was P.M.S'ing or just in her feelings but she felt like getting some shit off her chest. She felt like raising some hell.

"So, I'm not gettin' nothin' for Mother's Day?" She questioned with an attitude.

"Mother's Day has come and gone. What you talkin' about?" Tyreik focused on the game.

"I know that but don't you think it's fucked up that you didn't get me anything?"

"No, you ain't my mama. We ain't got no kids together. Remember, you took care of that." Tyreik flicked the ashes from the blunt into the ashtray.

The air in Chyna's lungs almost fully depleted. *Did this muthafucka really just say that to me?*, she thought. What he'd said was technically true but for years he always said he looked at India like she was his. Yes, when she was 17 she'd aborted their baby. Chyna just wasn't ready at the time. She'd thought that she would've gotten pregnant again by now but nothing ever happened. She didn't know if it was God or her ovaries that was holding her up from getting pregnant.

"That's a fucked-up-ass thing to say." She swallowed the huge lump in her throat.

"It's the truth." Tyreik said not backing down.

"So now you don't look at India as being yours?"

"I mean, I ain't tryin' to be funny or nothin', but she's not. You and I both know that she barely even likes me."

"And I wonder why?" Chyna shot furiously. "I wouldn't like you either if I was her. Look at how you treat me."

"Man, don't start. I'm not in the mood. I'm tryin' to play the game." Tyreik responded becoming heated.

"I don't give a fuck about you or that game! I wasn't in the mood when you ruined Mother's Day for me!"

"Let you tell it, I ruin everything. What about all the good shit I do for you?" He placed the game on pause.

If she wanted to go there, then Tyreik was ready to have the conversation.

"Don't none of that count for nothin'? You always bringing up the bad shit I do. What about when I massage your back, cook dinner or when I help you with your books? None of that matters, right? The everyday, little shit I do don't mean shit 'cause I ain't get you a punk-ass Mother's Day gift? Get the fuck outta here wit' that bullshit." He flung the remote control across the room.

"You know how basic you sound right now? Bitches out her dying to be in yo' position and you got the nerve to sit up here and complain." He eyed her with contempt.

Stunned by his choice of words, Chyna glared at him speechless.

"You have disrespected me on soooooo many occasions this year it ain't even funny." She finally spoke up. "You up here callin' yo' ex, not coming home at night, lying about who you wit', forgetting to think of me on holidays and let's not forget that yo' ass ain't lifted a finger to a pay bill in this muthafucka! You walk around this muthafucka like you King Tut and shit!" Chyna bobbed her head back and forth like a ghetto girl.

"And ain't got shit! If it wasn't for me, yo' ass would be homeless. So check yo'self, homeboy. 'Cause I don't know what world you living in!"

"You love being able to say that shit, don't you?" Tyreik mean mugged her. "Well, I got some news for you. I just had a phone interview with General Motors earlier today. I wasn't gon' say shit to you until I reached the third part of the interview process, but since you wanna be on some ole petty shit, I figured I'd let you know!" Tyreik exclaimed ready to choke the shit outta her.

"Mmm… good for you. 'Bout time you got off yo' ass and tried to get a job," Chyna shot back.

"Nope." He stood up. "I'm not about to do it. You not about to ruin my night. I'm not about to argue wit' you.

You can argue by yourself." Tyreik turned off the TV and walked upstairs to their bedroom.

"No! You gon' hear what I got to say!" Chyna followed behind him.

She'd completely blacked out. She didn't care that India was in her room and could probably hear their entire conversation. Some hard truths needed to be said.

"I'm about to go to bed." Tyreik yawned, unfazed by her dramatics.

"You won't be sleeping up in here until you listen to me," Chyna snapped.

"Chyna, go sit down. Don't you get tired of being mad and upset all the time?"

"That's a question you need to ask yourself 'cause you always doing something to piss me off."

"I ain't did shit to you, so you mad at yo'self." Tyreik threw the covers back.

"I'm not playin' wit you. You not going to sleep." Chyna flipped the covers back.

"Will you gon' somewhere? You doing too much."
He pushed her away aggravated.

"Are you ever going to propose to me?" Chyna
asked out of nowhere.

"What?" Tyreik looked at her in disbelief.

He was absolutely certain she was having a
psychotic break.

"You heard me." Chyna placed her hand on her hip
and stood back on one leg.

"Why would I propose to you? Look at how you
actin' right now. You won't even let me go to sleep," he
stressed.

"'Cause I can't ever get a straight answer outta
you!"

"Have you ever thought that maybe I don't have
any to give to you?" Tyreik got into bed.

"You not going to bed!" Chyna forcefully ripped
the covers off of him. "If you wanna go to sleep, you better
do it somewhere else."

"What the fuck is wrong wit' you? I keep tellin' you to gon' but you steady tryin' to start shit! Now if I slap the shit outta you I'll be wrong!"

"I just want you to understand how I feel," Chyna pleaded.

She urgently needed him to see that she was crying out for help. She needed him to save her from the pain that tormented her heart day and night. Each day that passed by she was leaking unseen blood. Soon she would die if things didn't change. She was tired of playing the crying game. She couldn't breathe and he didn't even know it.

"I know," Tyreik sighed staring up at the ceiling. "You mad 'cause I ain't get you a Mother's Day gift. If it'll make you happy and get you the fuck out my face so I can go to sleep, I'll by you a damn gift tomor."

"First off …fuck you," Chyna threw up the middle finger. "And it's more than that, Tyreik."

"Oh, and you mad 'cause I'ma piece of shit." He shot mockingly. "I don't ever do nothin' right. I'm such a horrible person. I'm always hurting you. Blah-blah-blah…blah-blah-blah-blah."

It took everything in Chyna not to grab something and hit him over the head with it.

"You can't sit up here and tell me that you don't see how your actions affect me. A relationship shouldn't be like this," she stressed.

"Why is everything my fault? What the fuck do you do? You don't think you get on my fuckin' nerves? Oh, I forgot; you're perfect. You're an angel." Tyreik came to the conclusion.

"Compared to you I am!" Chyna exploded. "If I did half the shit you do it would'a been a wrap!"

"Yeah, a'ight...," Tyreik scoffed. "Deep down you a monster too. You sit up there and whine and complain about the shit I do but you still here. So what that say about you? Maybe I'm not the problem. Maybe I'm not as bad of a person as you paint me out to be."

"I never said you were a bad person. You did." She corrected him. "That's how you feel about yourself. I just think you do some fucked up shit. I'm tired of wondering constantly about what you're doing, who you're with, if you're going to come home drunk and start a fight with me. I'm tired of constantly being let down by you."

"If it's that bad, then stop fuckin' wit me!" Tyreik challenged fed up. "Ain't nobody puttin' a gun to yo' head. Go out there and find somebody else. See how these other niggas out here treat you. You ain't gon' find nobody better than me. If you think I'm bad, these niggas out here are ten times worse. I love you." He pointed to his chest furiously.

"I ain't gon' get the boyfriend of the year award but I treat you good. I ain't going upside yo' head. I ain't beating yo' ass. I try to be there for you and your daughter as much as I can but nah, that ain't good enough for you. Fuck with another nigga and see what you get!"

Chyna shook her head. Tears flooded her eyes. She was drained. She didn't have any fight left in her. The hole in her chest was eating her alive. It was becoming clearer and clearer that she and Tyreik would be better off apart. He didn't appreciate her or anything she did. She was over pretending that she was happy. She wasn't. Faking it didn't seem appealing anymore. She had to leave him alone.

Tyreik ran his hand across his head frustrated. He didn't know what to say or do. He was sick of always having to prove himself to her. She didn't appreciate anything he did. He'd done everything he could to show her how much he loved her. Chyna was never satisfied. She always had something to say. Whenever she didn't get her way she started fights and threatened to put him out. That shit was old but Tyreik could never just stand there and watch her cry.

"Come here, man." He went and stood before her.

He hated to see Chyna cry. He never wanted to be the cause of her pain. He had to make things right with her. They'd come too far to give up now. Chyna sobbed like a baby as Tyreik took her into his strong arms. The smell of his cologne captivated her. Swaying from side-to-side, Tyreik made her slow dance with him. He pressed the side of his face against hers. With his lips up to her ear, he sang softly.

"We've had our problems, baby...Mmm... But we still made it through...We've been through the storm, suga.... Yes we have but I'm still in love with you... I see the pain, baby, deep in your eyes, even though you're smiling... I know it's hard and it feel like we fell out of love... But, baby, hold on 'cause we've come too far."

There was no way he was going to let her slip away. Everything they'd been through they'd been through for a reason. Their hardships only made them stronger. With time, they'd get it right. Tyreik knew he had some major things that needed to be changed. He was doing the best he could. Chyna had to realize that her expectations of him might not always match up to who he actually was. Tyreik was set in his ways. He wasn't looking to change everything about him to satisfy Chyna's needs.

Chyna listened as he sang. Normally, she would've melted but not this time. Tyreik didn't get it and he never would. It wasn't about her finding somebody else. She just wanted him to acknowledge her feelings. Each day that passed, the hope she had for them was beginning to fade. She felt like her insides were about to rot. She couldn't cry, yell, argue, plead, beg or compromise anymore. Her patience was wearing thin.

She wore the pain she carried on her sleeve for the world to see. It amazed her that Tyreik didn't notice that she was falling apart at the seams. She never wanted the love of anyone as much as she wanted his. Loving him had become an addiction. The more he disregarded her feelings, the faster she crawled back for more.

Only he could fix the hole in her heart. Only he could stop the numbness. Why couldn't he keep his word and love her like he'd promised? Or was this all he had to give? Chyna couldn't continue to be their life boat. She couldn't hold herself, him and her daughter together. She was only one person. She could only do so much. She was tired of being his savior. This time, she needed him to save her.

"I DON'T WANT TO MOVE TOO FAST
BUT... CAN'T RESIST YOUR SEXY ASS."

-ANDRE 3000, SPREAD

CHAPTER 13

A black blindfold covered Chyna's eyes. Anticipation filled her veins. She didn't know much except that she was in the backseat of a Rolls Royce. Chyna arched her back as Tyreik caressed her thigh. The intoxicating smell of his cologne and friction he was stirring in her pussy was driving her mad. She didn't care that it had taken her two hours to get dressed. Her big, black, voluminous curls, vibrant, yellow, bandage dress with a peek-a-boo cut out under her breasts, and nude, Louboutin '*Pigalle*' heels could all go. She would gladly get naked if he asked her to. Tyreik placed his lips up against her ear and nibbled on her earlobe.

"Baby." Chyna purred turned on. "Where are we going?"

"I gotta surprise for you." He ran his tongue across her neck.

Chyna tasted like candy.

"You better stop before I take this blindfold off and show you how a grown woman gets down."

"Open your mouth," Tyreik said in a low, raspy tone.

Chyna parted her lips hesitantly.

"You bet not put your dick in my mouth," she warned. "If that's your plan, give a girl a heads up."

"Just do it." Tyreik laughed.

Chyna opened her mouth wide. An assortment of grapes brushed up her lips. Chyna licked one then took it into her mouth. The sweet nectar from the grape splashed in her mouth as she chewed. Tyreik swept her hair to the side as the car hit a bump in the road. It was taking all of him not to devour her. Chyna resembled a work of art. Her sex appeal was on another level. The tight fabric of her dress clung to her breasts causing her hard nipples to protrude. He wanted nothing more than to run his tongue across the exposed part of her skin.

Chyna was dangerous and she knew it. Tyreik watched as her wet tongue danced with eagerness inside her mouth. She wanted to taste him. He could tell. For months Chyna had wanted him to pay attention to her. Now that she had his undivided attention she wasn't going to let it go. He could rip her dress off, smudge her lipstick, she didn't care. She wanted all of him. Her body craved him.

"Baby, fuck me," she begged.

Tyreik loved when she talked nasty. His dick was brick hard.

"Not yet." He traced her lips with his chocolate covered thumb.

Chyna hungrily took it into her mouth and sucked. If he was going to torture her by making her wait, she wasn't going to make the decision easy. Slowly she glided her sticky tongue across her upper lip. For a second, Tyreik thought about telling the driver to pull over so he could have his way with her. But both of them had no choice but to behave. Their ride to the undisclosed location had ended. They were finally at their destination.

Tyreik took Chyna's small hand and led her out of the car. Nervous that she was going to fall, she took baby steps as she walked. After what seemed like forever, they stopped. Standing anxiously, Chyna held her breath as Tyreik untied the blindfold.

"Surprise!" Everyone yelled as she opened her eyes.

A look of shock and awe was etched on her face. Chyna didn't understand what the party was for until she looked around. Huge posters and stacks of her latest book, MG3, filled the space. The book cover was plastered on a banner, cake, cookies, and napkins. There was a DJ, strobe lights, white, leather, rental furniture, an ice sculpture, buffet, cigar roller and a photo booth. All of her family and friends were there. Everyone from her mom and dad to Asia and Jaylen was in attendance. Tyreik had even made it open for her readers to attend. The place was filled to capacity.

"You did this?" Chyna asked befuddled.

"Yeah, I wanted to make it up to you for not getting you anything for Valentine's Day or Mother's Day," Tyreik explained. "I apologize, again, baby. The way you look after me and India - you deserve this and even more."

Tears stung the brim of Chyna's eyes. This was all she'd ever wanted - recognition. All she wanted was for Tyreik to acknowledge all of the heartache and sacrifice she'd endured. She wanted to know that it was all worth it, that he cared. In that moment, she was proud to be his girl. There was good inside of Tyreik.

She wished he would show that side of him more often. Maybe then she wouldn't be on edge all the time. Chyna wrapped her arms around his neck and basked in his presence. Her heart hadn't been this full in a while. She wanted to ask where he'd got the money to throw such a lavish party but kept her mouth shut. She didn't want to ruin the moment. Tyreik was looking waaaaaay too good. She needed him inside her desperately. If she had to wait much longer, she would have to start without him.

It wasn't until after hours of dancing, hundreds of pictures and numerous glasses of champagne that she got her wish. They sky was dark and full of stars. The sunroof on the Rolls let in a warm, summer breeze. Tyreik and Chyna sat in the backseat as the driver navigated his way down Highway 70.

Sex was in the air. A yearning for Tyreik simmered through Chyna's veins. She couldn't contain herself as she unbuttoned his jeans. His dick was rock hard. Tyreik reached inside his boxer/briefs and pulled his dick out. The 10 inches of pure chocolate bliss in his hand looked like heaven on a stick. As the moon eavesdropped from up above, Chyna took him in her mouth inch by inch until he filled her up.

Into an ocean of love they both feel. Tyreik closed his eyes and relished the feel of her tongue as she swallowed him deep. The tongue lashing Chyna was putting on his dick almost made him weep. He was almost sure that by the time she was done satisfying him there would be no evidence that he ever existed. Inhibited, Chyna found her rhythm. She didn't know what it was but her body was in deep need of a different kind of drug.

Tyreik was the perfect remedy. Deep down she knew the high she experienced was temporary. Tyreik always knew how to reel her in and temporarily satisfy her needs. Chyna was no dummy. When it came to Tyreik, disappointment was inevitable. It was just a matter of time before he made her cry.

Tyreik wouldn't act right for long. Every fiber in her being screamed he'd fuck up again. She prayed it was all in her head but Chyna wasn't the silly, wide-eyed girl she used to be. As soon as she let down her guard he'd get too comfortable and shatter her dreams of a happily ever after. But Chyna didn't want to concentrate on that. At that moment, she was willing to take whatever she could get. Fuckin' him would fill the hole in her heart that he'd left behind.

"ALL BITCHES WANNA DO IS START SHIT AND SAY I'M TOO PRETTY TO BE FIGHTIN'." – SOURCE UNKNOWN

CHAPTER 14

The whole crew was posted at the Delmar Restaurant & Lounge. Thursdays at the Delmar Lounge were always lit. The crowd was a mixture of hipsters, thugs, THOT's, vagrants and drunks. There wasn't much to the décor. Everything was made out of mahogany wood. They sold an array of different liquors. There Cajun themed menu was some of the best in the Lou.

Chyna, Brooke, Kingston and Juelz sat in a booth in the back of the lounge. Chyna sat in the booth by the window. Brooke sat beside her. Kingston and Juelz sat across from them. It was a rarity that everyone got together and kicked it. It sucked that Tyreik wasn't there to share in the turn up. He was at home. His third and final meeting with GM was the following morning. Chyna couldn't have been prouder. She was happy to see things finally coming together for him.

This was the confidence booster Tyreik needed. Chyna wasn't worried at all. She knew he was going to land the job. She was honestly over the bar and ready to go home. Snuggling up in bed with him seemed way more enticing than being in a bar filled with drunks. Since Tyreik wasn't there she was going to celebrate in advance for him. Drinks and laughter flowed all around.

Chyna didn't really care for Kingston but she couldn't front. Homeboy was a good time. He stayed buying drinks and everybody in the place wanted to be around him. Kingston was a ladies' man. Chicks were always in his face trying to get at him. He and Brooke at one point tried to date but they were too much alike. Neither could tame the other. Now they were good drinking buddies who flirted.

Outside of celebrating Tyreik's upcoming deal, Chyna was in a celebratory mood because of the release of MG3. For the most part, the book had received good reviews. Chyna was pleased with the outcome considering the stress she was under while writing it. If only her readers knew all she had to go through to write a decent piece of work. It was hard creating characters that only existed in her mind. She had to give make-believe people an entire life when she could barely manage her own.

It was growing increasingly difficult to outdo herself, especially when her love for the craft was wavering as time went on. Chyna was starting to feel unfulfilled. Dealing with shiesty publishers was starting to wear on her.

With all of the blood, sweat and tears she'd put into her work, she shouldn't have to fight tooth and nail for a royalty check she was rightfully owed.

The only things that kept her going was the fact that writing was her livelihood and the love of her supporters. She wanted something different. She just hadn't figured out what that something different was yet.

"Brooke, you lookin' kinda right tonight," Kingston eyed her lustfully.

Brooke wore a low-cut top that revealed much of her breasts.

"Get yo' life. I'm always lookin' right." She rolled her neck. "It ain't my fault you want a taste."

"I'ma get it too." He winked his eye.

"You just might." She flirted back.

"Ewwwww," Chyna pretended to throw up. "Stop! I'm gonna lose my lunch."

"Chyna, you the biggest hater ever." Kingston screwed up his face.

"No, I'm not. I just don't wanna see you two flirt about you lickin' her vag."

"Chyna, I bet you a prude in the bedroom. You probably check yo' watch while you and Tyreik fuckin'," Juelz teased.

"If I'm lookin' at my watch, that mean yo' boy ain't doing something right," Chyna checked him.

"Ok!" Brooke gave her a high-five.

"Sex-wise men are only obsessed in three things anyway. Your rocket launchers," she squeezed her boobs. "Home base," She pointed to her vagina. "and for some odd reason, your calve muscles, hence my all purpose, come fuck me pumps." Brooke kicked out her leg.

"Speaking of my boy, I'm mad he couldn't come out tonight." Kingston took a swig of his beer.

"You keep him out enough." Chyna griped, rolling her eyes.

"What's yo' problem wit' me?" Kingston leaned forward and frowned.

"You ain't shit," she replied bluntly.

"Damn, that's how you feel?" Kingston questioned perturbed.

"You know I don't like you and you know why I don't like you," Chyna reminded him of a past incident.

"Shit, I wanna know too," Brooke laughed, looking back and forth between them.

Chyna ignored Brooke and continued on.

"Tyreik and I are in a relationship but you still be tryin' to keep him out in the streets like he single. That ain't cool," Chyna stood her ground.

"You do realize that I ain't puttin' a gun to that nigga head? Tyreik a grown-ass man. He do what he wanna do. And if I ain't shit, then why I throw your book release party for him? Hell, technically, I'm your boyfriend," he shot.

Chyna sat speechless. She wondered how Tyreik was able to throw her the party. Never in a million years did she think Kingston was the one behind it. She was still happy that Tyreik had done something to appease her but it sucked to know that he had to go to another man for help to do it. It was also a let down to know that once again, Tyreik hadn't used his own resources to do something for her. He could buy clothes, buy new rims and tires but when it came to Chyna, she was always an afterthought.

"That's what's up and I appreciate it." She pretended like she knew what was going on.

"Y'all made a lot of money too that night," Juelz bigged Kingston up.

"Wait a minute. Y'all charged people at the door?" Chyna asked confused.

"Hell, yeah. I had to make my money back. I wasn't doing that shit for free. You ain't my girl. After I made my investment back, me and Ty split the door," Kingston confirmed.

Chyna was pissed. Tyreik had conveniently neglected to tell her any of this. *Once again this nigga is hiding money from me,* she fumed. *And ain't gave me a dime!* It angered her to the core that he'd used her readers to make a profit. Chyna hid her displeasure. She didn't want her friends to know she was upset. Kingston could tell she was upset though.

"You gotta learn how to chill, ma," he continued. "You gon' fuck around and have a stroke."

"Why I gotta chill?" Chyna turned up her face. "I ain't the one always fuckin' up."

"'Cause look… you mad now. Tyreik a good dude, man. He don't be on no shit for real."

"But I know you've heard the saying, 'who you surround yourself with says a lot about you'," Chyna opposed. "Tyreik ain't got no good influences around him. He needs to be around married men so he can get marriage on his mind."

"Get the fuck outta here." Kingston waved her off. "You can't talk. Look who you hang around." He pointed at Brooke.

"What the fuck is that supposed to mean?" She interjected.

"Right! She don't try to get me to cheat!" Chyna refuted his claims.

"But she still not a good influence." Kingston raised his brow.

Chyna knew he had a point but she would never admit it. Her feelings towards Kingston would never change.

"You gotta fall back and let that man do him."

"And what that mean?" She rolled her neck.

"A man gon' be a man, Chyna," Kingston stressed leaning back. "You can't keep tabs on that man 24 hours a day. Let that man do him."

"And by doing him, what do you mean, cheat?" She died to know.

"Now see, I ain't even say all that."

"What he's saying," Juelz chimed in. "Is that a man gon' fuck up from time to time. That don't mean he don't love you."

"Both of you niggas sound fuckin' crazy," Chyna exclaimed.

"That's real talk. As long as that man taking care of home you good. Tyreik love the fuck outta you. He say it all the time but do you know how much ass get thrown at that man on a daily basis? Shit, you can't turn down everything," Kingston added.

"So you sayin' Tyreik cheating?" Chyna repeated.

"You stay on that cheating shit." He cracked up laughing. "I see why that nigga be spazzing out on you."

"No, that's what it sound like you sayin'." Brooke spoke up.

"If he was cheating, do you really think I would tell you?" Kingston quizzed.

"See, that's why I cheat!" Brooke downed her shot. "Fuck giving yo' heart to these niggas. Ain't none of they asses about shit. I love my nigga to death but you'll never catch me without options. You can't focus your attention on one man. You'll lose yo' fuckin' mind. I'm tellin' you, being faithful gets you nowhere."

"I don't agree with that," Chyna objected. "If you gon' cheat, then you might as well be single. I ain't tryin' to be out here fuckin' this nigga and that nigga."

"Yeah, 'cause you still over there chasing after a house wit' a white, picket fence. You still believe in fairytales. I don't. A woman in love is like a helpless dog.

Her tongue is always hanging out slobbering. It's not a pretty sight."

"So how do you feel about soul mates?" Chyna inquired.

"I think the shit is overrated," Brooke replied.

Chyna sat quiet. She felt sorry for her friend and the guys at the table. She didn't understand how they'd become so desensitized to love. What happened to building a family? They had to want to grow old with someone. Bouncing from dick to dick and fuckin' this chick and that chick had to get old at some point.

Not having a true connection with someone wasn't the way to live. People were put on the earth to love, mate and marry. The Bible said, "he who finds a wife finds a good thing". These dudes now-a-days didn't realize that having a good woman by their side was a blessing not a hindrance. If they only allowed themselves to love wholeheartedly and be loved, they'd see that.

Chyna felt the reason Brooke thought the way she did was partly her fault. When they were younger, Chyna did the unthinkable and smashed Brooke's first love. Ever since then, Brooke hadn't been the same. She forgave Chyna but her heart had grown cold.

Over the conversation, Chyna took a sip of her Amaretto Sour. Out of nowhere she began to feel uncomfortable. An eerie sensation surrounded her. A bad feeling crept in her stomach. Goosebumps covered her arms. Something was about to go down. Sitting up straight, she surveyed the room.

Checking her surroundings, she spotted the devil herself. Rema walked through the crowd as if she owned the place. Chyna's stomach immediately began to hurt. She hadn't seen the bitch in years. A lot had changed about Rema. She was no longer the beautiful chick she used to be.

She was dusty as hell. It looked like she smelled like falafels and fungus. Life had done a number on her. Homegirl wasn't cute at all. Her lips were black from smoking too much weed and she didn't wear the right foundation shade. Her body was insane though. Rema's shape reviled Amber Rose or Emily B but she had a gut. She didn't feel no type of way about wearing a skin tight, puke green, satin, Bodycon dress. Her flabby stomach jiggled as she walked and Chyna noticed that her heels were leaning to the side.

Despite all of her flaws, Chyna could see why Tyreik would still be into her. He liked big booty, ghetto bitches like her. Rema may have been competition for Chyna back in the day but she sure as hell wasn't now. Chyna ice grilled her as she approached their table. Brooke turned and looked at her to see if she was good. She wasn't. Chyna's face burned red. Down for whatever, Brooke cocked her head back and shot Rema a death glare.

Rema leaned down and asked Kingston in his ear, "Where Tyreik?"

She made sure she asked loud enough so that everyone at the table could hear. Chyna blinked her eyes and placed her hands up in the air.

Did this chick really just ask where my man was, she thought on the verge of losing her shit.

"He at home." Kingston looked over at Chyna nervously.

He knew she was crazy and would set it off in a minute.

"See, this what I be talkin' about. He be on some bullshit. He told me he was gon' be here tonight" Rema said, flushing in distress.

"Oh she tried it." Brooke took off her earrings.

She may not have liked Tyreik but she would always have her best friend's back no matter what.

"What you mean he told you he was gon' be here?" Chyna stood up.

"Girl, sit down," Rema waved her off dismissively.

"On my mama. On my daughter, I will fuck you up," Chyna warned looking up at the sky.

"Bitch, please; you ain't gon' do shit!" Rema talked with her hands. "You ain't gon' touch me."

"Don't put yo' hand up, bitch, 'cause that could get you popped!" Chyna stressed bobbing her neck.

"Girl, whatever! I'm too old and too pretty to be fighting." Rema flicked her long, 32 inch weave to the side.

"Bitch, where?" Chyna looked her up and down. "You look like a laundry bag full of Play Station 2's!"

"You's a dumb bitch. Now I see why that nigga stayed at home. Look at how you act," Rema pointed. "Don't nobody wanna be around you. You do too much. Learn how to play your fuckin' position," Rema snapped.

"Oh, I see this bitch wanna box!" Chyna reached across the table to hit her but missed.

"Chyna, chill!" Juelz tried to push her back down into her seat.

"No, this bitch obviously wanna catch the fade!" Chyna tried to get up again.

"Ay yo, Rema. You gotta go," Kingston urged pushing her away.

"Yeah 'cause best believe as soon as she swing again I'm coming right behind her." Brooke shot ready for war.

"Girl, bye." Rema rolled her eyes, flicked her wrist, then walked away.

"That bitch got me fucked up!" Chyna yelled mad she wasn't able to hit her.

"No! Fuck that!" Brooke pounded her fist on the table causing their drinks to shake. "Yo' nigga got you fucked up! Why are they even still communicating?" She questioned, heated.

"You don't know that," Kingston tried to defuse the situation.

"C'mon man, don't try to play me like I'm dumb," Brooke snapped. "The bitch just said he told her he was gon' be here."

"Right!" Chyna agreed pulling out her iPhone.

"That don't mean shit. She could be lyin'," Juelz reasoned.

"Bullshit, that bitch ain't lyin'."

"Chyna, what you doing?" Juelz asked as he watched her fingers move quickly over her screen.

"I'ma beat his ass." She hissed, texting him.

<Messages   **Tyreik**   Details

When I get home, I'm fuckin' u up!!!!!

183

"Man, chill 'cause that nigga ain't coming to my crib tonight," Kingston said with a laugh.

"Take me home!" Chyna shot up, grabbing her purse.

"Oh Lord, here she go." Kingston feared for his friend.

"You damn right! Here the fuck I go!"

"YOU THINK THE DEVIL IS A LIAR. YOU MUST'VE NEVER MET A NIGGA FROM ST. LOUIS." —SOURCE UNKNOWN

CHAPTER 15

The entire ride home all Chyna could think was telling Tyreik the fuck off. For months he'd been treating her as if she was paranoid and crazy. He had her really doubting herself. She didn't know why she'd been waiting for some type of physical proof to fall into her lap. She knew her suspicions were right. Tyreik wouldn't be able to lie his way out of this. She wouldn't let him.

Hysterical, she ran up the steps. Her heart was racing a mile a minute. She had no control of her emotions or herself. A sick ache filled her stomach. Chyna didn't care that it was the middle of the night and that he and India were asleep. Her psychotic alter ego had entered the building.

Blinded by rage, she switched on the wall light, threw her purse on the floor and walked over to him. She hated the sight of his face. How dare he sleep peacefully while her heart broke into a million different pieces? *I wish that you were me so you can feel this feeling,* she thought.

What had she done to deserve the pang in her chest? It wasn't fair that she was the only one hurting. He had to feel the pain too. He couldn't get away with treating her like shit. If she was going to suffer, then so was he. Rearing her hand back, Chyna slapped the shit out of him. The force of the hit caused him to jump out of his sleep.

"What the fuck?" He woke up holding his face. "What the fuck you hit me for?"

"You are fuckin' wit' that bitch!" Chyna yelled.

"What the fuck are you talkin' about?" He shot her a look that could kill.

It was apparent by the bewilderment on his face that he hadn't gotten her text.

"Rema! She was lookin' for you tonight." Chyna took off her earrings, necklace and watch prepared to fight.

Tyreik's eyes darted back and forth frantically. He didn't know what Chyna had been told so he didn't respond right off the bat. He didn't want to incriminate himself.

"I'm so sick of you lyin' to me. Do you get some kind of sick pleasure out of doing this to me? Like, what the fuck." Chyna tried to steady her breathing. "Just admit it! You fuckin' wit' the bitch!"

"I don't even know what you're talkin' about." Tyreik threw his thick, long legs out of the bed.

All he wore was a pair of Calvin Klein boxer/briefs.

"You come in here at 1:00 in the morning on some bullshit and you know I got my interview in the morning! That's some fuck shit!"

"Fuck all that." Chyna waved her hand.

"We was at the Delmar and Rema come up to the table asking Kingston where you was at. Like y'all together. He told her you were at home. Then here she come talkin' about you be on some bullshit. 'Cause apparently you told her you would be there tonight. So you still hittin' this raggedy-ass bitch up after you said you erased her number?"

"You sound so fuckin' stupid. Why would I tell someone I'm going out tonight if I got a job interview in the morning? Do you think?"

"Do you ever stop lyin'?" Chyna pushed his forehead back with her index finger.

"Keep yo' hands to yo'self!" Tyreik grabbed her hand and threw it back. "'Cause if I hit you back, I'ma knock yo' ass out!" He ice grilled her.

"You ain't gon' do shit!" Chyna stepped out of her heels ready to bang.

"MOM!" India said at the bottom of the steps.

"What is it, India?" Chyna's chest heaved up and down.

"Can you guys please be quiet? I can hear you all the way downstairs."

"I'm sorry, baby. Go back to bed," Chyna ordered.

Once the coast was clear, Chyna zeroed back in on Tyreik.

"You done starting shit and raising hell 'cause I gotta get up in the morning?" He asked.

"Yo' lyin' ass ain't stayin' up in here! Go sleep at that bitch house," Chyna tried to block him from getting in the bed.

"Get yo' crazy-ass on some where." Tyreik pushed her away with his elbow.

Chyna stumbled back almost losing her balance.

"I ain't going nowhere. How the fuck you gon' try to put a nigga out and I been in the house sleep? You the one who been out in the club all night! You always wanna talk about me and how I ain't got no job, now I'm tryin' to get one and you tryin' to fuck that up. Coming in here on some punk-ass bullshit. Lay yo' ass down and go to bed!" Tyreik shot irritated beyond belief.

Once more he went to lie in bed but Chyna stopped him by snatching all of the covers off the bed.

"You think it's a game? I'm done doing this shit wit' you! You not gon' continue to play me like I'm stupid," she cried.

"Really, Chyna?" Tyreik looked at her like she was dumb. "You cryin' 'cause a female asked where I was at while you was in the club? Are you serious right now?"

"Damn right, I'ma feel some type of way when a bitch walk up to yo' pot'nah while I'm sitting right there and question him about your whereabouts. That shit ain't ok." She wiped her face. "Her whole reason for being there was to see you."

Tyreik could see that Chyna was on her last leg. She was unraveling right in front of him. It scared him. Angst ridden tears dripped from her dimpled cheeks. He had to do something to soothe her fears.

"Babe, it ain't nothin' like that. You trippin'. You blowing things outta proportion, as always." Tyreik held her by the arms. "You know how hoes are. That could've been her sparking up a conversation to get at him. Hell, they could be fuckin' around for all I know."

"Ok, Tyreik." Chyna angrily pulled away from his embrace. "Alright. Now they fuckin' around? Sure. Tell me anything. Pass them the juice."

"Why you letting this bitch fuck wit' yo' head? Can't you see she just don't want us to be together?"

"Uh ah! Hold up." A thought came to Chyna's mind. "Fuck talkin' about that bitch. Let's talk about this party."

"What party?"

"The book release party you threw for me. So Kingston paid for everything? Then y'all charged people at the door and split the profits?"

Tyreik massaged his jaw. *Fuck, she knows,* he thought.

"Yeah, nigga, you ain't think I was gon' find out, did you? That's lousy. How I'ma have a book release party and you charging people at the door? You know how that makes me look? If it wasn't for my readers you wouldn't have shit. Profiting off my hard work and ain't gave me shit. Where they do that at?"

"That's apart of party promoting. We gotta make a profit somehow," Tyreik tried to reason.

"Just fuck it." Chyna threw up her hands fed up.

"You don't get it. I come at you on some you need to be more romantic 'cause you ain't did shit for me all year long type shit. Then, you throw me this surprise book release party and I'm here thinkin', 'ok, he finally stepping up to the plate'. But noooooo the party wasn't even about you doing something special for me. It was about you using my name to make money but ok, I'm crazy." She gave him a mock-glare.

Chyna held her head and willed herself not to drop another tear. Her entire body was hot with anger. He was literally driving her insane. She could see how women flipped and killed their spouses. Tyreik was the worst. The lines of what was reality and what was fake was starting to blur. Who should she believe: Rema, Tyreik or herself?

What she and Tyreik were doing was nothing more than child's play. She was sick of being the brunt of his joke. She hated him yet loved him all at the same time. But she couldn't keep being on the losing end of the stick. She had to learn how to let him go, but the thought of living a life without Tyreik was unfathomable. There was no Chyna without him. He was a piece of her but she couldn't believe his lies anymore. She had to see things for what they were.

"I can't do this no more." She bit into her bottom lip as tears slipped down her face and fell onto her shirt.

"C'mon, man; stop." Tyreik tried to hold her.

"You ain't gon' never change. You gon' keep on doing the same shit over and over again," Chyna sobbed uncontrollably. "I can't keep letting you run over me." She wiped snot from her nose.

"Babe, ain't nobody tryin' to run over you."

"You got me out here lookin' stupid than a muthafucka. I know people be out here laughing at me 'cause they know you a user," Chyna spat.

"Is that all you care about is what other people think?" Tyreik made her look at him. "Do you think I'ma user? You don't think I love you? You don't think I wanna spend the rest of my life wit' you?"

"Why even go through this? You know I ain't got nobody. You all I got. You all I need. You all I want. It's us, baby. Fuck all that other shit." He tried to make her see.

"Just do us both a favor and leave 'cause I ain't tryin' to argue wit' you around my child," Chyna ignored his cries and pushed him off her.

"I'm not going nowhere."

"Tyreik, just leave, please. I can't think straight when I'm around you." She massaged her temples and paced back and forth across the room.

"Like, ain't you tired? Don't you get tired of hearing me complain? 'Cause I'm tired of hearing myself fuckin' complain."

"You can be mad all you want to but no, I'm not leaving this time. You can either get in bed and go to sleep or stand there and be mad. It's on you. Either way, I'm going to bed." He fixed the covers.

"See, that's what I mean. Why won't you just stop? I keep on asking you to stop doing this stuff to me and you just keep on doing it. Which only tells me that you don't give a fuck. And you know why you don't give a fuck? 'Cause you don't respect me. You think you can do what you want and I'm just supposed to put up wit' it. That's not how life works. I'm not letting you get away with this shit this time. I'm done. I'm not doing this wit' you no more," she stressed.

"So that's it? You just gon' break up wit' me like that? It's that easy for you? You know I ain't got nobody but you. You all I got, Chyna. What I'ma do without you?"

"You should've thought about that before you lied," she frowned.

"Oh word? It's like that? You really gon' put me out over some bullshit? Where the fuck I'ma go?" Tyreik yelled.

Chyna hung her head and groaned. When shit got real, Tyreik always tried to throw a guilt trip on her. He always tried to make it seem like he was the victim. It wasn't her fault that his mother was dead or that his father was serving a life sentence in jail. If family meant so much

195

to him, if it was so important, then maybe he should've acted like it.

"Go to Rema's house," she replied coldly.

"That's fucked up and you know it." Tyreik felt his self becoming emotional.

He didn't know what to do. He hadn't seen Chyna this distraught in a while. Maybe this time he'd pushed her too far. Yeah, he did a lot of questionable things. Sure, he'd hurt Chyna too many times to count but he meant it when he said she was all he had. Without her, he'd shrivel up and die. Chyna was his anchor. She grounded him. She gave him purpose. He never wanted to see a day where she wasn't in his life. She was all he knew.

The pain he was in was evident. A small tear had formed in his eye. Chyna began to feel bad about her response but what she'd stated was true. Tyreik would always land on his feet. He'd lived without her before. She was sure he'd be able to do it again.

"Please, just go," she begged.

She honestly didn't have anymore fight left in her.

"Chyna, just lie down." Tyreik pleaded desperately.

Seeing that he wasn't going to budge, Chyna nodded her head.

"A'ight." She licked her bottom lip.

Since he wouldn't leave, she decided she would. She didn't want to be near him.

"Where you going?" Tyreik asked as she descended down the steps wearily.

Chyna didn't bother to answer. She wasn't going to give him anymore of her energy.

"Chyna!" Tyreik called out again helplessly.

Ignoring him, Chyna walked to India's room. Her sweet baby was sound asleep snuggled underneath her covers. It had been ages since she slept in the bed with her daughter but that night Chyna needed to be surrounded by real, genuine love. Quietly, she slipped under the covers. She lie curled up in a ball next to her daughter. She was mentally, physically and emotionally drained. She couldn't take another day of the back and forth bullshit between her and Tyreik. The nigga had to leave.

"IF YA' MAN DON'T BE STRESSIN' YA', NEED TO COUNT YA' BLESSINGS." –FANTASIA, ONLY ONE YOU

CHAPTER 16

"Mom." India gently shook her mother's arm.

It was mid-afternoon and her mother still hadn't woken up. Chyna needed all the rest she could get after the night before. Going through emotional roller coasters with Tyrcik exhausted her. Chyna's eyes instantly fluttered open.

"Huh?" She shielded her eyes from the sun.

The sun was beaming in her face. Chyna was a light sleeper but she hated being woken up. If you bothered her while she was asleep, she was sure to go off.

"When did you get in my bed?" India asked lying beside her mother.

Chyna turned her head to the side and removed her hand from her face. She couldn't contain her smile. She loved her daughter so much. Waking up to India's adorable face made her heart sing. Chyna reached over and ruffled India's unruly, curly hair. She sometimes found herself in awe of what she'd created. India was a young lady now. She was wise beyond her years. She was oftentimes more mature than her mother.

"When you gon' let me flat iron your hair?" She pulled at one of India's curls.

"Mom, focus." India pushed her hand away. "You and Tyreik were fighting again."

"No we weren't. We were having a conversation," Chyna lied.

"Really, Mom?" India twisted her mouth to the side. "Then why are you in my room?"

"'Cause I wanted to sleep with you." Chyna tickled her stomach.

Chyna might've thought she could fool India but India was smarter than Chyna thought.

"Mom, stop!" She laughed uncontrollably.

"Ok-ok." Chyna ceased tickling her.

Once India calmed down, she instantly became serious.

"Mom, can I tell you something?" She looked down at her hands timidly. "And you gotta promise you won't get mad."

"India, you can tell me anything. I won't get mad."
Chyna's heart raced. "You can tell me anything." She
prayed to God that nothing bad had happened to India.

She didn't want to have to kill somebody, let alone
go to jail.

"What's wrong?" Chyna sat up on her elbow.

"I don't like Tyreik. I want him to go," India
confessed hesitantly.

"Why?" Chyna's heart dropped.

"'Cause y'all always fighting and I don't like how
he talk to you. You always sad and crying all the time. It's
better when it's just me and you here."

"I know you don't like when we fight and I'm sorry
when you have to hear us. But no relationship is perfect,
love. You're going to argue sometimes."

"But y'all argue all the time," India countered.

"I know, but you won't understand until you get
older and get into a relationship. Relationships are hard
sometimes. Adults fight and when you love someone
sometimes your emotions can get in the way and rile a

person up. When you get older you'll see what love can do to you. But besides that, Tyreik loves you."

"No he don't," India quipped. "He barely even talks to me. The only time he communicates with me is when we're all together."

"Now, India, you act like he don't help you wit' your homework and try to talk to you about school and stuff."

"He only helps me wit' my homework because you suck at math. He don't love me. He loves you."

Chyna would never admit it because admitting it would mean facing reality but every word India spoke was true. India and Tyreik really didn't have a relationship. It came across like India was an accessory to Chyna. Tyreik didn't treat them as if they were one. It was more about Chyna than India. She wanted India to feel loved by Tyreik, especially since her real father was no where around.

When India was around six she started to ask questions about her father. She started to notice that other kids had dads and she didn't. Chyna would never forget the day India asked her about her father. It was the middle of winter. She and India were at the grocery store. India was in the cart bundled up. They were in the meat aisle. Chyna was picking up a pack of ground beef when India asked out of nowhere, "Mom, why don't I have a dad?"

Chyna swore her heart stopped beating. She almost dropped the pack of ground beef. Chyna caught her breath and looked around the grocery story. She hoped no one had heard. Once she saw the coast was clear she exhaled. She'd been dreading this day since the day India was born. She thought she had prepared herself for such a question but now that the moment was here, she was speechless.

"Ummmm," she held the ground beef in her hand. "I don't know baby."

That was all she could tell India because she honestly didn't have the answers. The door for LP to be in India's life was always open. He just never chose to walk through it. She'd heard through the grapevine that he was balling out of control. His drug empire was the biggest in town now that Tyreik had retired. He'd married a stripper and had a slew of other kids. It baffled Chyna that a man could be so rich and not pay the $150 a month child support ordered on him.

He never once reached out to see India. Hell, for all he knew, she and Chyna could be dead. Chyna didn't know how he was able to rest his head at night knowing he had a child in the world that he didn't take care of. Chyna didn't want to, but after India begged to see her father, she reached out to him. After years of not communicating, she and LP talked. He was just as dumb as Chyna remembered. She even let him speak to India over the phone. Chyna never saw India happier. A joy filled her face as she heard her father's voice for the first time.

Chyna and LP made plans to meet up at McDonald's so he could see India. She asked him to call her when he would be on his way since she would be coming in a cab. On the day of the meeting, Chyna and India sat on Chyna's bed fully dressed awaiting his call for hours. When India realized he'd played her and wasn't coming, she broke down and cried into her mother's arms like someone had died. Chyna had never witnessed that kind of pain and agony ever from a child, especially hers.

For years she'd tried her best to shield her child from any sort of pain. On that day she failed. From that day forward she vowed to never allow her daughter to hurt like that again. Nobody would ever make her feel small or unwanted. Chyna went above and beyond to show her daughter that she was loved. She and India did everything together. They had mommy/daughter day where they would watch movies, go shopping, go out to eat, visit the library. You name it, they did it.

Chyna was determined to fill the void in her heart of her father not being around. But deep down inside, Chyna knew that a young girl needed a father. Chyna's father wasn't 100% in her life growing up and it affected her greatly. Chyna didn't want the same for her daughter. She wanted India to know what it felt like to have a mother and father in the house.

"I'm sorry you feel that way, baby." She took India in her arms and held her close.

She felt like an absolute failure as a mom. She'd done everything in her power to be a better mother to her daughter than her mother and father was to her. But here she was, fucking her child up equally as bad. She had to make a decision and quick. She would be a pretty shitty mother if she kept a man around that her child couldn't stand. On the flipside, she couldn't live her life for her child. She had to have a piece of happiness for herself too.

"Mama loves you. You're my heart and soul, my greatest accomplishment. You know that, right?" She looked India square in the eye.

"Yeah." India nodded her head.

"So you really want him to leave?" Chyna whispered.

"Yeah."

Chyna inhaled deep.

"Ok… when he gets back from his interview I'll tell him he has to go."

"For real?" India said eagerly.

Chyna could see the hope in her eyes.

"Yeah. If you don't want him here, then he gotta go. Now let me go brush my teeth." She eased out of bed.

"Yes, please. Yo' breath is on 100," India joked.

"Just for that, I'ma let him stay!" Chyna threw a pillow at her before running out of the room.

Feeling confident about her decision, she jogged up the steps. She damn near fell back down the stairs when she spotted Tyreik sitting on the edge of the bed smoking a blunt. She just knew he was gone.

"Boy, you scared the shit outta me." She held her chest. "What are you doing here? Why ain't you at your interview?" She walked past the bed and over to her closet.

"I stayed here to talk to you."

Chyna's heart skipped a beat. She couldn't believe that he'd missed the biggest meeting of his life for her. That still didn't change anything. He had to go.

"You shouldn't have did that. If you can still go, you better." She shot sarcastically.

"Can you sit down for a minute?" Tyreik said in a somber tone.

"Yeah, 'cause I need to talk to you anyway." Chyna sat opposite him on the bed. "Listen—"

"Nah, let me go first." Tyreik cut her off.

"Mmm… excuse me," Chyna smirked.

"I ain't get no sleep last night—"

"Am I supposed to feel sorry for you?" Chyna cut his sentence short.

Tyreik cut his eyes at her.

"I couldn't sleep 'cause I was up thinkin' about you," he admitted.

"Is that right?" She laughed.

Tyreik paused. The tears in his throat were inhibiting his speech. He was overcome with emotion.

"Listen, I'm not tryin' to lose you," His voice quivered.

Is this nigga about to cry, Chyna wrinkled her brow.

"Chyna, you are my life. What we got is real. You know that. Me and you gon' get married and have a couple of kids. You're my fuckin' wife, so ain't no breakin' up. We're in this forever. And I know I've been fuckin' up lately but on everything, I'm tryin' to get it right. I'ma do better. I swear," Tyreik said sincerely.

"Ain't gon' be no more arguing and fighting. We gon' talk to each other calmly. I ain't gon' stay out late.

I'ma spend more time with India. I'ma fall back on going out and everything. We can make this work, babe. You know we can." He took her hand in his.

"Baby, I love you. If I lose you, I don't know what I'ma do."

Chyna looked down as their fingers intertwined. Her honey-colored skin glowed against the darkness of his hand. She'd been here so many times before with Tyreik. He'd promise he'd change and she'd naively believe him. Chyna couldn't continue to play herself. Tyreik was probably spitting game, but this time, something inside his eyes told her that he was telling the truth. There was a sincerity and desperation there she'd never seen before. He truly was afraid to lose her.

Yes, she'd promised India that he would be gone but India was 13-years-old. She didn't know anything about love or loving a man no less. Chyna would explain to her that things were going to change. The non-stop bickering was done. India would probably be mad at first but after a little time passed, she'd become comfortable with her mother's decision. She and Chyna would be good. At least that's what Chyna told herself.

"Ok." She said softly. "But if one more thing happens, I'm done for real."

"Ain't shit gon' happen. I swear." Tyreik pulled her into his embrace.

Holding her tight, Tyreik thanked God that she'd given him another chance. He couldn't tell her that the real reason he didn't go on the interview was because he couldn't risk coming home and not having a place to stay. He loved Chyna, he did, but Tyreik was his own worst enemy. He wanted to do better but he just didn't know how.

He always got in his own way. He didn't deserve her. She was too good for him and he knew it. Tyreik would always be one step behind Chyna. He didn't like the fact that she didn't need him. He felt like she was the man of the house. She basically took care of him.

He would never live up to her expectations but he didn't want anyone else to have her either. He couldn't let another nigga take a sample of the woman he'd invested so much time into. He'd practically raised her from a pup. No, he would tell her what she wanted to hear. Once things died down, he'd go back to doing him. 'Cause there would never be a day where Chyna wasn't his. They would be together forever or until the day he died.

"I KNOW THAT'S YO' MAN', HO.
HE AIN'T GOT NO BANDS, THO." –
TINY & SHEKINAH, CUT IT OFF

CHAPTER 17

Life for Chyna seemed like a step and repeat cycle.
Every other day was like Groundhog's Day. She and Tyreik
hadn't argued in a few weeks but the tension was still there.
They barely had anything to say to each other. Chyna just
wasn't feeling it anymore. The sight of his face annoyed
the fuck out of her.

Every time he entered a room she became anxious.
She felt crowded, like she couldn't breathe. She needed her
space. She wanted to tell him to leave but knew he didn't
have a place to go. It wasn't helping that he was living
there and not bringing any money into the house. He would
go to the Dollar Store and buy toiletries but hell, India
could do that.

She needed him to step up to the plate and pay the
gas or electric bill or hell, both. She was tired of seeing him
sitting around soaking up her good air and her good,
premium package, cable. Tyreik was starting to become
one big disappointment to her. She almost wanted him to
go back to selling dope but she wasn't about that life
anymore.

She most certainly didn't want that shit around her daughter. Something had to change quick. Her home was starting to feel like a prison instead of a place of relaxation. Nobody was happy. They all walked around like zombies.

India barley had two words to say to her after she reneged on putting Tyreik out. Chyna felt like shit. She was a dirtbag and she knew it. She hadn't figured out how she was going to fix things with her daughter. Not repairing their relationship wasn't an option. India was her world. Chyna always came through in the clutch. Somehow she'd make it alright.

Needing some form of release, she hit Brooke and Asia up. It was almost the end of August. Asia was in town for another month. Chyna wanted them all to go get matching tattoos. Asia was hesitant on getting tatted. She was a tattoo virgin and swore she'd never get inked. But she couldn't be left out of the best friend tattoo session.

That Saturday afternoon the girls hit up Chyna and Brooke's favorite tattoo parlor. Trader Bob's Tattoo Shop was the shit. It was located on the Southside of St. Louis. All of the tattoo artists were kind and friendly. Everyone made you feel welcome. The vibe was very laidback and chill.

After much chatter and bickering, the girls decided on getting a bow with cheetah print inside. Brooke went first and got hers on her right shoulder. Chyna went second. As soon as the needle hit the skin of her inner wrist, she regretted the decision. It had been a few years since she last got tatted. She'd forgotten how painful the process was. Once it was over she thanked God and swore never to get another tattoo. She and Brooke sat on a bench, bandaged up, while Asia took her turn in the chair. A look of absolute dread was plastered on her face.

"You'll be ok, girl. It don't hurt that bad," Chyna assured. "Labor pains are way worse."

"Oh ok." Asia perked up feeling better.

"Y'all wanna go eat after we leave here?" Brooke asked, rubbing her stomach.

She was always hungry. Chyna secretly hated that she could eat so much and never gain weight.

"Hell yeah," Chyna answered always down to feed her face.

"That's cool. Jaylen got the baby so I'm straight," Asia assured. "Oh and I heard about you clowning at the Delmar a few weeks ago." She looked over at Chyna.

"That bitch started with me. She tried my life and when you try my life, my man or my child, I'ma fuck you up," Chyna said indignantly.

"Yeah she tried it but didn't Tyreik try it first when he talked to her?" Asia quizzed.

Chyna shot her a look that said 'really bitch'.

"I mean, I'm just sayin'," Asia raised her brows. "Seems to me like yo' nigga the problem not her."

"He the common denominator," Brooke chimed in while checking her Instagram.

"He said he ain't fuckin' wit' her so what else can I do?" Chyna shrugged her shoulders frustrated.

She did not come out to talk about Tyreik all day. She wanted to get her mind off of him. Plus, she was tired of defending their relationship every five minutes.

"Anyway, we should go to the Rustic Goat tonight. They having something there," Brooke suggested.

"I might be down," Chyna said.

"I'll have to see. I think I wanna stay in tonight with my man and my baby," Asia blushed. "Did I tell y'all that Aiden is crawling?" She inquired.

"You told me," Brooke replied.

"You ain't tell me." Chyna turned her face and looked away, mad.

"I thought I did but you over there runnin' from Ike, Anna Mae. Half the time you don't even answer the phone." Asia half joked as the tattoo artist switched on the machine and pricked her skin.

"Oh shit! Fuck! I thought you said it wasn't gon' hurt that bad," she winced.

"That's what yo' ass get." Chyna hit her with the middle finger.

"I'ma beat yo' ass when he get done. Watch." Asia threatened trying to keep her composure.

"But for real, that's how y'all look at me?" Chyna died to know.

Brooke and Asia side-eyed each other before speaking. Neither of them felt like wasting their breath when it came to the subject of Chyna and Tyreik. They'd had the conversation at least a million times and she never listened. They were over giving her advice. It was apparent that she liked being mistreated and used.

"Uh ah, don't be side-eyeing me. We do that to other people. We don't do that to each other." Chyna stomped her foot, hurt.

"I'm not about to have this conversation wit' you no more." Brooke crossed her legs with an attitude. "It is what it is at this point. I've come to the conclusion that when you're done being abused, you'll leave."

Chyna swallowed hard. She hated that her friends looked at her like she was weak. But she was when it came to Tyreik. He was her soft spot.

"I think that's a bit much. I'm not being abused," she disagreed. "We only got physical with each other once and that was years ago."

"Chyna…,"Brooke whipped her head in her direction.

"Brooke, chill." Asia tried to interject before she flipped out.

"Nah, she need to hear this." Brooke didn't give a damn that they were in a public place. Her friend needed some tough love and she was the perfect person to give it to her.

"Just because he ain't going upside yo' head don't mean you not being abused. He stay fuckin' wit' yo' mind. Shouldn't no man feel comfortable callin' you out yo' name. He forever fuckin' up shit 'cause he jealous of you. All that nigga got is a closet full of clothes, half of which you bought. You over there takin' care of him, India and you. That nigga don't contribute shit but some good dick," Brooke shot heated.

"And good dick don't pay no bills," Asia added.

"But he help out around the house," Chyna tried to explain. "He's always cooking us dinner."

"YEAH, WIT' YO' FOOD!" Brooke stressed, flabbergasted. "That's the least that nigga can do, especially since he ain't payin' no bills. He don't get brownie points for that. And the only reason he cook for y'all is 'cause the nigga hungry and he gotta eat. You better wake up, girl. You better see this shit for what the fuck it is. As much as you do for that muthafucka, you need to be claiming him on yo' taxes at the end of the year."

Chyna tried to refute Brooke's claims but couldn't. She was right.

"It's just hard 'cause I love him and he ain't got nobody but me. I just can't up and leave him. He was there for me. I just can't say fuck him when he down."

"And why not?" Brooke cocked her head to the side. "'Cause trust and believe if the situation was reversed, he wouldn't hesitate to leave you. Let me put you up on game." She situated herself in her seat.

"I can't say whether or not he love you but I can tell you that part of the reason that nigga is wit' you is because he need a place to stay. If that nigga had his shit together he would've been gone."

"You really think so?" Chyna barely spoke above a whisper.

"Yes. Tyreik was a hustler. He gone always be straight; believe that. Don't let that nigga fool you with that sob story. Tyreik gon' always be straight. He gon' always find a place to lay his head."

"I hear you, Brooke, I do; but you just don't understand. It ain't that easy. I've been wit' that man since I was sixteen."

"Ok, girl, if you say so," Brooke became frustrated and gave up. "That's on you. Don't come crying to me when he fuck up again."

Chyna tried her best not to cry. The tears were on the verge of falling *Don't you shed one tear,* she held her breath.

"You can come cry to me, friend." Asia poked out her bottom lip sympathetically.

Chyna looked over at Brooke. Neither of them could help but burst out laughing. Asia was an idiot.

"She can come cry to me too. She just get on my damn nerves." Brooke wrapped her arm around Chyna's neck and hugged her. "You know I only want the best for you, right?"

"I know. I'ma get it together one day."

"Lord knows I pray you do 'cause you dumb as hell," Brooke made fun of her.

"Right," Chyna concurred. "If my readers only knew how dumb I was, I wouldn't sell no damn books."

"ONCE YOU LET A MUTHAFUCKA SLIDE, THEY START FIGURE SKATING." –SOURCE UNKNOWN

CHAPTER 18

Chyna's girls' day with her besties was exactly what the doctor ordered. When she was with Asia and Brooke, a good time was always had. Chyna laughed until her stomach was sore and ate till her belly was full. By the time she got home later that afternoon she was spent. She'd begun to feel sick. She felt like she was coming down with a cold.

She was pleased as punch that Tyreik wasn't there when she got home. She needed a minute to herself to gather her thoughts and take some meds. Her friends had laid some serious shit on her at the tattoo parlor. Thankfully, India had eaten dinner and was occupying her time by playing Call of Duty with other online gamers. Chyna had a chance to take a shower, lie under the covers and get her mind right.

The TV was on. She watched an episode of Marrying the Game. Chyna watched The Game's fiancée, Tiffany, try on wedding dresses with dreams of one day being in a wedding gown of her own. From the time she was 16 she'd envisioned herself walking down the aisle to Tyreik.

He was her first love, her everything. She'd never felt a love like theirs before. No matter what they went through, they always found their way back to each other. That had to count for something, right? Tyreik wasn't the best man but he wasn't the worse either. He loved her. She knew that for sure but what Chyna was starting to realize was that maybe the love they shared wasn't healthy.

Chyna didn't know much about relationships except from what she'd seen growing up, the movies she watched and what she read in books. She thought arguing was a natural part of a relationship that everybody did. No couple on earth was happily in love all the time. They all went through shit.

She figured if after their battles they came back to one another, then they were meant to be. No matter what she did to Tyreik or what he did to her, they always ended up back in each others arms. Yes, they'd hurt each other in unimaginable ways but their love outweighed the tough times. She was made to be with him and vice versa.

As Chyna lie in bed feeling like death, she heard the sound of Tyreik's heavy footsteps come up the stairs. Chyna reached over on the floor and grabbed a cough drop. Her throat was killing her. She low-key couldn't wait to show him her new tattoo. Tyreik climbed the steps one- by-one slowly. Once he entered the bedroom Chyna turned and looked at him with a smile on her face. Her smile quickly faded when she saw how drunk he was.

His eyes were bloodshot red. It wasn't even 7:00pm and he was already lit. The excitement to show him her tattoo was gone. When Tyreik was like this it was best to stay clear of him. Chyna turned her attention back to the television without saying a word. Tyreik stared at her then grinned. It was amusing to him that she wasn't going to speak.

Nodding his head, he held the crotch of his dark denim, Levi jeans and stumbled into the bathroom to take a leak. Tyreik peed for what seemed like hours. He didn't even bother to close the door when he did. When he was done peeing he walked over to the sink to wash his hands. He was so fucked up that he knocked over the soap dispenser and the tooth brush holder.

"Fuck! My toothbrush just fell down the sink!" He yelled, trying to dig it out to no avail.

Chyna glared at the TV annoyed. He was making so much noise. She could barely hear the television. It was obvious that he was trying to get her attention by any means necessary.

"Baby!" He stepped out the bathroom. "My toothbrush just fell down the sink."

"Did you try to get it out?" Chyna replied, not bothering to give him eye contact.

She was trying to keep things as peaceful as possible but she knew by Tyreik's mind state where the conversation was heading.

"Yeah, I can't get it. Come do it for me."

"I don't feel good, Tyrcik," she sighed.

"What's wrong wit' you?" He leaned up against the doorframe to give himself balance.

"I'm coming down with a cold." Chyna sat up on her elbow and rested her chin in the palm of her hand.

"You can't come do that for me tho?" Tyreik shot her a devilish glare.

"No, you can do it yourself. I don't feel good."

"But I do stuff for you all the time," he argued.

Chyna knew he was trying to bait her into a fight. She wasn't in the mood for it.

"Ok," she chuckled, focusing on the television show. "We not gon' even go there."

"So, I don't do shit for you?" Tyreik scowled.

Instead of replying, Chyna continued to watch TV. She wasn't about to argue with him.

"I cook and clean around this muthafucka like I'm the female. While you lay up on yo' fat ass not doing shit!"

Chyna's eyes grew wide. *Did this nigga just call me fat,* she thought. *Did he really just go there?* Unwilling to fight, she lay quiet.

"You know it's the truth. That's why you not sayin' nothin'. You can't come get a toothbrush out the sink for me when I missed my whole job interview for you?"

So that's what his problem is. Tyreik blamed her for not getting the job at GM. She wasn't the one that told him not to go. He made that choice on his own. Keeping her composure, Chyna continued to ignore him. She prayed he'd get the hint and go somewhere and sit down until he sobered up.

"Oh, so you gon' act like you don't hear me?" Tyreik stood beside the TV stand. "For real? That's how you do me? So you gon' act like you don't see me standing here?" He placed his hands in front of him.

Chyna acted as if he didn't even exist.

"You's a silly bitch. You know that? Just basic and dumb. I don't even know why I fuck wit' you." He spewed words of venom. "I don't even like you. I tolerate yo' ass. Shit, yo' own daughter don't even like you."

Tyreik was going to do whatever he could to get a reaction out of her. He wanted her to feel the rage he felt on the inside. Chyna took her eyes off the TV and finally gave him eye contact.

"That got yo' attention." He mean mugged her.

For the first time when Chyna looked into his eyes, she didn't see love or compassion. She saw nothing but hate. She was never afraid of Tyreik but that day she was unsure of what he might do.

"You don't respect me. You treat me like I'ma li'l loc. Remember it was a time you ain't have shit and I took care of you."

"That was how many years ago?" Chyna finally shot back.

"I don't give a fuck how long ago it was! It happened!" Spit flew from Tyreik's mouth. "You making a li'l dough now and think you top flight. That li'l money you makin' ain't shit! You ain't betta than me!"

"The li'l money I make feed and clothe yo' broke-ass!" Chyna spat. "So you can gon' with that. I'm not about to argue wit' you. You drunk. Get away from me." She shoo'd him away like he was a fly.

"Who you think you talkin' to? I ain't some li'l ass boy! You don't shoo me away!"

Chyna inhaled deep and rolled her eyes. If Tyreik wanted to argue, he would have to do it alone. He wasn't going to suck her into his madness.

"On everything I love you ain't gon' sit there and ignore me." Tyreik clapped his hands.

Unfazed by his antics, Chyna yawned and continued to watch Marrying the Game. Tyreik licked his bottom lip. He realized that he wasn't going to get a rise out of her with his words. He'd have to do something drastic.

"A'ight. fuck you then." He barked, taking his hand and pushing over her TV.

Before Chyna knew it, her flat screen was falling over. She could hear it crack and break into a million pieces as it hit the hardwood floor. For a second, she lie there in complete shock. In the past she would've reacted instantly by yelling and screaming. She probably would've even tried to attack him. But that day, she didn't have the fight in her.

A stream of tears strolled down her checks as she pulled the covers back and got out of the bed. Chyna worked too hard for her shit for him to be fuckin' up her stuff. She didn't care that her feet were barc and that there was shattered pieces of glass all over the floor. Tyreik stood by the door as she lifted the flatscreen off the floor.

"Why would you do that?" She asked distressed. "I didn't do nothin' to you." She cried so hard she could barely see.

"You shouldn't have been ignoring me. I tried to get you to talk to me," he replied nonchalantly.

"So you break my shit?" Chyna's voice cracked.

"Mom, is everything alright?' India rushed into the room."I heard a loud bang downstairs."

India got her answers when she saw her mother's broken TV.

"He broke my TV." Chyna tearfully replied.

"Why?" India looked back and forth between them as her mother continued to cry.

"I don't know. You have to ask him." Chyna tried to make believe that it was all a bad dream.

But it wasn't a nightmare. This was real life. Once again, Tyreik had betrayed her trust. She was starting to realize that she couldn't trust him with anything. Nothing was safe with him. Not her heart, their relationship, her child, her house or her things. The nigga simply didn't give a fuck. He couldn't be trusted.

"That's why she don't like me now 'cause you always putting her in the middle of stuff! That's why her ass so grown now! She need to stay her ass in a child's place! This between me and you!"

"What the fuck you mean this between me and you?" Chyna spazzed out. "I ain't do nothin' to you! You came here starting shit 'cause you feelin' some type of way! It ain't my fault that you haven't amounted to shit! It's not my fault that you're an irresponsible, selfish, alcoholic, drunk! You're a bum! You're a bum-ass nigga!"

"I wasn't a bum when I was putting this dick up in you!" Tyreik shot back.

"Watch your fuckin' mouth! Don't you see my daughter standing here?" Chyna pointed at India.

"She'll be a'ight!" Tyreik waved her off. "Don't act like this shit is new!"

"I fuckin' hate you. I swear to God, I do. You ain't shit." Chyna shook her head in disbelief.

"I ain't shit? Look at you! You one cheeseburger away from having a heart attack!" Tyreik exclaimed.

He knew that talking about Chyna's weight would get under her skin.

"Have you looked at yourself in the mirror lately, my nigga? You wear the same shit over and over again! You got on a thousand dollar outfit and ain't got a pot to piss in! Who's fault is that? Yours! Not mine! Everything you got, nigga, I bought! Everything you want, nigga, you lookin' at me to get! You ain't shit! You wack! You lame as fuck! So since you wanna go around breakin' shit, take yo' clothes out my fuckin' closet and get the fuck out!"

"MAN FUCK THAT!" Tyreik picked up one of her scented candles and threw it. "I ain't going nowhere! You ain't puttin' me out!"

"Oh, you ain't gon' leave?" Chyna called his bluff and grabbed her phone. "Ok." She dialed 911.

India stood quiet in the middle of room unsure of what to do. She'd begged her mother to make him leave but she didn't listen. If she had, none of this would've ever happened.

"Hi, can you send the police to 901 Allen Avenue. My ex," she emphasized the word ex. "Just broke my television and is refusing to leave my house."

"That's some fucked-up-ass shit! You wanna see me locked up just 'cause I broke yo' li'l punk-ass TV? That's foul than a muthafucka! You ain't shit, bitch!"

"Tyreik, fuck you. Just take the shit I bought you and go," Chyna rolled her eyes holding the phone.

"What you bought me?" He looked her up and down with disgust. "I don't give a fuck about what you do for me or what you bought me! What you could buy me! What you planning on buying me! I don't give a fuck about none of that! You think this material shit makes me?" He eyed her with disgust. "Any shit you do for me another bitch will do for me ten times better!"

"Ok then, nigga," Chyna took the phone away from her ear. "Since you don't give a shit about none of the stuff I did for you, then leave everything I fuckin' bought you where it's at! All you got is that muthafuckin' car outside wit' the gas I put in that muthafucka! Nigga, fuck you! Where yo' gas money at?" Chyna rolled her neck.

"Oh, I forgot you ain't got none. Broke-ass! Get the fuck outta here!" She placed the phone back up to her ear. "And leave that fuckin' toothbrush. I bought that too!"

"That's all you care about is what you do for me! I swear to God on my mama, I ain't never fuckin' wit' yo' childish-ass again! You a fuckin' kid. Ain't no nigga gon' ever put up with the shit I put up wit'. You a kid. Grow up, bitch!" Tyreik opened the closet door and began to pack his things. "Fat ass ho!"

"Can you send someone quick? I don't feel safe and I have my daughter here," Chyna tapped her foot on the ground repeatedly.

The words he was hitting her with stung like bee stings.

"Now you don't feel safe around me?" Tyreik stopped packing and charged over to her.

In her face he yelled, "I've been around her since birth but now you don't feel safe? You wanna sit up here and play me like I'm some psychopath! That's why I been fuckin' Rema this whole time! You stupid bitch!" He mushed her in the head.

Chyna almost dropped the phone. He'd finally admitted what she already knew. Tyreik knew exactly how to hit her where it would hurt the most. He wasn't going to leave until he emotionally assassinated her. Chyna refused to let him see her break down. It was bad enough India was crying. She felt helpless.

"It's ok, love. Everything is gonna be alright. The police are on the way." Chyna assured, holding her daughter tight.

India wrapped her arms around her mother's waist and clung on for dear life.

"Let's see if the police gon' hold you at night or cook for you! You gon' regret this shit! I swear to God you will!" Tyreik grabbed all he could before the police arrived.

He had a ton of tickets and was way over the legal drinking limit. If the police arrived while he was still there, he was sure to be arrested.

"You gon' regret this shit!" He pointed his finger at her like a gun before leaving in a rush.

Chyna didn't let out a sigh of relief until she heard the front door slam shut.

"SOMETIMES I FEEL SO STUPID FOR TEXTIN', ESPECIALLY WHEN YOU DON'T BE REPLYING." – STACY BARTHE, TOUCH

CHAPTER 19

Three weeks had gone by since Television Gate. Tyreik came back a few days later to pick up the rest of his things. When he walked in he apologized for breaking her TV and promised he'd give her back her key. After that, he proceeded to pack his stuff in silence. Since then she hadn't spoken to him once. He hadn't returned her key nor bothered to replace her flatscreen.

She'd called him more times than she could count about the matter. Tyreik ignored each and every call. The calculated disrespect drove Chyna mad. He'd fucked up her shit, and yet and still, he treated her feelings with disregard like she was the culprit. She swore Tyreik was bipolar. Something had to be clinically wrong with him and her too. This breakup was much like the last time they'd broken up seriously. She'd put him out and he'd given her his entire ass to kiss.

Chyna was a complete and utter fool for him. Although he did nothing to better her life, facing the future without him was a scary fete. Bad or good, he was all she knew. The ill, sick feeling that took over the pit of her stomach whenever he wasn't around had started to rear its ugly head. Crying, praying or ignoring it wouldn't make it go away. Only Tyreik could make it disappear. He was her only cure.

Yes, he'd acted an ass but after much thought, Chyna came to the conclusion that his outburst was a cry for help. He needed her in that moment to boost his ego and tell him that everything would be ok. It had to be hard being with a woman that made more money than him. Tyreik was used to being the bread winner. Over the years, he'd become a kept woman.

Somehow he'd lost his way. He needed Chyna to lift him up and guide him in the right direction. Instead, she totally disregarded him. She should've seen he was in desperate need of saving. She hadn't though and now she was all alone. She wasn't having it. She was 31-years-old. She and Tyreik had made it this far. There was no turning back now. She would be damned if she was going to give in and say fuck it.

She'd be damned if she let him walk away without trying to save their relationship. Tyreik would change. Once he got on his feet and built a career for himself, he'd act right. It would be them against the world. Chyna was not about to lose her man. She was not going to face another tearful night alone. She needed him there with her. The TV could be replaced; he couldn't.

Chyna sat on the floor dressed in one of his old tee shirts that he'd left behind. Her back rested against the side of the bed. Going against her better judgment, she picked up her phone and dialed his number. She didn't even realize she wasn't breathing until he forwarded her to voicemail. Chyna shook her head. When he wanted to be, Tyreik could be so cruel. She wasn't about to give up. She was going to call him until he answered. Chyna dialed his number again and was forwarded once more to voicemail. This time she left a message.

"Tyreik, I need to talk to you. Pick up the phone, please." She said then hung up.

Chyna didn't waste anytime calling back. The cycle of her calling and him sending her to voicemail continued for over two hours before Tyreik gave in and answered.

"What?" He responded exasperated.

"You busy?" Chyna asked eagerly.

"Yeah, what's up?" Tyreik spoke in a dry tone.

"I need to talk to you."

"About what? We already talked that day you put me out, remember?" He shot.

This nigga love to hold a grudge, she thought.

"Tyreik, you were acting crazy. What did you expect for me to do? Just let you cuss me out and break my shit for no reason?" She spoke stunned by his ignorance.

"Is that what you called me for? 'Cause if so, I'ma hang up on you." Tyreik replied arrogantly.

Chyna knew she shouldn't have let him talk to her that way. She wanted to have some pride and cuss his ass out but the pain in her chest outweighed her self-respect. She would rather beg and plead for him to come home. Chyna swallowed any dignity she had and said, "I called 'cause I want you to come home."

Tyreik couldn't help but laugh.

"You do this every time. You wanna run and tell somebody to get out, then after a few days you realize what you've done and be over there sick, begging me to come back. Why the fuck should I come back? So you can get mad and put me out again?"

"'Cause we can make it work." Chyna pleaded hearing the desperation in her voice.

She didn't even recognize herself. She sounded like a lovesick puppy. She hated the sound of her own voice but she couldn't stop herself. She'd already fallen down the rabbit hole.

"I love you and I'm sorry for callin' the police. I overreacted. I shouldn't have done that."

"You damn right, you shouldn't have done it! It was stupid as fuck. If I would've got locked up then what? You ain't think about that shit! All you care about is that you mad! Well, I'm mad too! Now what?" He questioned perturbed.

"I'm sorry," Chyna wept.

She was so distraught she couldn't even think straight. She sat there on the floor and cried like a baby.

"Yo, you can save the tears 'cause I really don't care," Tyreik remarked repulsed by her tears.

"Will you just come home? I promise I won't do it no more," Chyna begged.

"You won't do what no more?" He quizzed.

It boosted his ego to hear her beg.

"I won't put you out or call the police. But you can't be around here tearing up my stuff. That ain't cool. It ain't right. I didn't do anything to deserve that."

"I already apologized for breakin' yo' shit. I ain't apologizing no more," Tyreik quipped.

"I'm not askin' you to! I just want you to come home!" Chyna wailed her arms frantically like a child.

"I don't know about that. I don't think that's a good idea," Tyreik sighed.

She was starting to make his head hurt.

"Why not?" Chyna asked, feeling herself fall apart.

"'Cause I'm tired of you naggin' me. You stress me the fuck out. Every time you feel some type of way you wanna put a muthafucka out. And let you tell it, I'm always cheating. That shit is for the birds. I'm good."

"You said it out of your own mouth that you were fuckin' Rema!" Chyna shrilled.

"You know damn well I was lying."

Chyna let out a huge sigh of relief. Her subconscious knew he was just telling her what she wanted to hear but Chyna would take whatever distraction from reality she could. Facing the truth was not an option.

"Why did you say it then?" She sniffled.

"'Cause you pissed me off," Tyreik barked.

"Baby, I miss you. I promise that if you come back, I'll change." Chyna said reducing herself to nothing.

"It's too late for that, man," Tyreik exhaled. "We just need to go ahead and leave each other alone. I can't keep putting myself in a position where I'm constantly being put out of a place I call home. I'm not going to do it no more. You ain't gon' ever be able to do that shit to me again. That's why I got my own crib."

Chyna damn near dropped the phone. Her head instantly jerked back. She just knew she hadn't heard right. *How did this nigga get his own crib*, she wondered.

"When did this happen?"

"A few days ago."

"I ain't even trying to be funny but... how?" Chyna declared taken aback.

"I called GM and told them that I had a death in my family. I told them that was why I missed the interview. They heard me out and gave me another date to come in. After the interview they hired me right on the spot."

"That's what's up. I'm proud of you. I knew you could do it." Chyna congratulated him.

She was happy for him. She couldn't even front though. A part of her felt like she'd been slapped in the face. It was funny to her that he took the initiative to run out and get a job and a crib when she put him out but the whole time he was there with her he was in no rush to better himself or help her out. She was instantly reminded of what Brooke said. *A nigga gon' always find a place to lay his head.*

"Look, I'll drop off yo' key either today or tomor. And when I get paid I'll get you another TV but other than that, I ain't got nothin' for you. I'm good."

"So it's like that? It's that easy for you to leave me? After everything we've been through?" Chyna began to tremble.

"You left me when you put me out."

"Yeah, after you broke my TV!" Chyna shrieked incredulity.

"You always gotta place the blame on me! You can't ever take responsibility for what the fuck you do! It's all good tho," Tyreik calmed down. "I don't even know why I'm raising my voice. That ain't even me. We ain't together no more so we ain't got nothin' to argue about. I'm about to be about my day. You have a goodnight." He hung up before she could utter another word.

Mentally, physically and emotionally broken, Chyna cried until her throat became sore. She cried so much her eyes were swollen. If she couldn't get Tyreik back on her own, then she'd go to a higher power.

"God, please." She begged as snot ran down her nose. "Bring him back. I can't be without him. I love him and I just want him back. Lord, please, I promise I won't fly off the handle. I'll listen before I react. I won't cuss him out or make him leave. I'll change, Lord. I'll be a better woman. Just please touch his heart. Let him see how much I love him. I can't do this by myself, God, please."

"I KNOW I WAS MAD, SAID I WAS PISSED BUT IT WASN'T SO BAD. NOT WORST THAN THIS." – LEDISI, I MISS YOU NOW

CHAPTER 20

The crazy had officially taken over Chyna. Once again, Tyreik had lied to her. A week and a half passed and he still hadn't dropped off her key or bought her a new TV. Plus, he'd gone back to ignoring her calls. Not being able to communicate with him was the worst feeling ever. Chyna found herself wondering what he was doing or who he was with. If Tyreik had started fuckin' with other females already she'd surely die.

She wouldn't be able to handle it. She needed advice. She couldn't go to Asia or Brooke for help. They'd laugh at her and tell her she had lost her goddamn mind. They'd probably even try to have her committed. Chyna was surely certifiable. The only other person she could trust to talk to was Jaylen. Although they used to have a thing and he was married to Asia, he was still one of her best friends.

She valued his opinion. He would never steer her wrong. After being in the house for what seemed like an eternity, Chyna met up with him at Mission Taco. Chyna was an avid lover of Mexican food. Mission Taco had some of the best Mexican food St. Louis had to offer. Located in

Soulard, the restaurant was made out of a restored brick building with giant garage doors that opened into an outdoor patio.

The restaurant had a cool atmosphere that consisted of an art mural and a great bar area. She and Jaylen sat a table for two enjoying a plate of carne asada fries. With Tyreik being gone, Chyna hadn't had much of an appetite. She'd lost ten pounds so her clothes weren't kissing her curves anymore. Jaylen tried not to stare at his friend but Chyna looked a mess.

Dark circles were around her eyes. Her skin was pale and she looked like she needed a good meal. He hadn't seen her like this since they were 17. The last time she looked this way was when Tyreik left her. He figured he'd left her again and that's why they were there.

"Talk to me. What's going on wit' you?"

Chyna gazed up at her friend wearily

Jaylen got finer and finer with age. That NBA money was doing him well. Diamonds gleamed from his ears, neck, pinky and wrist. Sometimes she wondered what life would've been like if she had given them a real chance. Jaylen was a good man. He was everything she prayed

Tyreik would be. He was smart, responsible, giving and attentive. He didn't lie or play games. He was a great husband and father. His and Asia's relationship proved to her that real love still exists.

"Me and Tyreik broke up again."

"Ain't this like the 1 millionth time?" Jaylen teased.

"Shut up." Chyna threw a fry at him. "I know it's ridiculous," she sighed.

"Y'all crazy. Me and Asia call y'all Whitney and Bobby," Jaylen laughed.

"I knew y'all be over there talkin' about me. What else y'all be sayin' about us?" Chyna quizzed.

"Not too much. We just wanna see you happy, that's it," Jaylen responded truthfully.

"I know you do. I want what y'all got. I wanna have a loving family and all that."

"We want you to have that. Nobody deserves it more than you. You a good girl, Chyna. And I ain't even tryin' to get all off into no Iyanla Vanzant bullshit but you could have it all if you truly believed in yourself."

Chyna looked down at her hands, embarrassed.

"You don't understand, Jaylen. He's not that bad. I wouldn't keep going back if he was." She tried to convince herself.

"And I understand that no relationship is perfect. Hell, me and Asia ain't perfect. We go through our shit too but we respect each other. We hold each other down. I would never disrespect her the way ole boy disrespects you. A real man don't cheat, cuss you out and tear up yo' shit. A real man provides and makes sure his woman don't want for shit. Does Tyreik do that for you?"

Chyna should've said no but she lied instead.

"He does when he got it." She couldn't even get the lie through her lips without almost choking on her words.

"So what made y'all break up this time?" Jaylen questioned, knowing damn well she was lying.

"He came home drunk, trying to start a fight and when I refused to argue back he broke my flatscreen. I told him to leave but he wouldn't so I called the police on his ass."

"Oh God." Jaylen placed his head down amazed by what he'd heard.

"After I had some time to think, I realized that he was mad because he'd missed his interview at GM. He just didn't know how to come out and say it. Long story short, he ended up getting the job and now he has his own place."

"And let me guess, you want him back but he ain't fuckin' wit' you?" Jaylen chuckled.

"You got it."

"Well, unlike yo' homegirls, I ain't gon' tell you to leave him alone 'cause that ain't none of my business. You gotta come to that conclusion on your own. When you're done, you'll know it. I will say that he was wrong as hell for breakin' yo' shit. Grown men don't go around breakin' shit." Jaylen stressed.

"I'ma keep it real wit' you tho. He broke your shit 'cause it ain't his. When y'all get into it you don't see him fuckin' up his shit, do you?"

"He ain't got nothing but his clothes, his shoes and his truck," Chyna rolled her neck.

"Exactly! That nigga ain't got shit to lose. You do. But, Chyna, you gotta stop calling the police. They be ready to kill a black man. Hell, they'll shoot yo' ass. They don't give a fuck about us. If your life and India life ain't in danger, then stop involving the police. Don't no black man, whether he legit or living dirty, want the police called on him. Shit, you put yourself in more danger when you call them muthafuckas."

"You're right and I already said I was gon' stop doing that. I just want us to try one more time. I feel like if I change the things about myself that need to be changed that we'll be straight. If shit don't work after that then cool, I'll let it go."

"I don't know why you think you're the problem but ok," Jaylen shrugged.

"I can be off the chain too, Jaylen," Chyna clarified.

"Oh, I know you crazy," Jaylen flashed a boyish grin.

"Look, if you want him back then shit… you gon' have to make your presence known. For a man, it's out of sight, out of mind. Find a reason to be around him. Wear something tight 'cause we like that shit. Put that colorful shit you girls like to wear on your face—"

"You mean makeup?" Chyna giggled.

"Yeah, that shit. Wear some of that. Be sweet. Don't be barkin' on him and don't be bringing up a bunch of old shit. We hate that. If you do all of that, he'll want that old thing back. But I'm tellin' you… that nigga ain't done fuckin' wit' you. He got yo' ass on punishment. He wanna make sure you never do that shit again. Once he think you've learned your lesson, he'll double back. He just tryin' to make you sweat."

"YOUR LOVE'S LIKE MY DRUG. I CAN'T LIVE WITHOUT IT." —TINK, MILLION

CHAPTER 21

Chyna took Jaylen's advice and ran with it. Since Tyreik wouldn't come to her on his own, she decided to lure him her way. Since it didn't seem like he was going to bite the bullet and replace her flatscreen, she called him and asked if he'd take her to go buy one. Tyreik agreed and came and picked her up. Chyna couldn't believe she'd stooped so low as to replace her own TV but she'd be waiting forever for Tyreik to do it.

It was obvious that he had no intensions of doing so. The least he could do was take her to the store. Plus, Chyna needed an excuse to be in his presence. As she walked outside to get in the truck she felt foolish for not making him pay for what he did. But she was in the thick of it. There was no reversing what she'd done.

After nearly two months, she finally got to see his face. Fall was making its presence known. The leaves had begun to change. Nightfall came quicker and the sun was hiding its face. Chyna switched to the car looking the best she had in weeks. She wore her silky black hair up in a messy bun. Her makeup was beat to perfection.

She wore a winged liner on her eye and M.A.C.'s Pure Heroine on her lips. A pair of gold, oversized, hoop earrings dangled from her lobes. Her outfit consisted of a hunter green blazer coat, white, strapless bustier that showcased her tone midriff, a pair of denim, booty shorts and brown, leather, gladiator, over-the-knee boots. Chyna was going to get her man back by any means necessary. The bronze body butter she wore gave her skin a honey-colored glow.

Tyreik couldn't take his eyes off her thick thighs. He'd forgotten how they felt wrapped around his waist. Normally, Chyna would've said something about having to open her own door but decided to take Jaylen's advice and keep it cute.

"Hi," she smiled cheerfully, climbing into the passenger seat.

"You do know we going to Wal-Mart, right?" Tyreik chuckled taking the car out of park.

"Yeah, I know, silly," she playfully hit him on the arm. "I gotta date after this." She placed on her seatbelt.

"A date, huh?" Tyreik sucked his teeth. "Why you ain't have that nigga take you?"

"'Cause he ain't break my TV. You did." Chyna shot unable to control her temper.

"I'm taking you to get a new one, ain't I?" Tyreik quipped, like it was some sort of consolation prize.

"That I'm paying for."

"I don't know if this is a good idea." He stopped the car in the middle of the street. "Maybe you need to find somebody else to take you."

"I'm already in the car; we might as well go. I'm not tryin' to spend my day arguing wit' you, so you ain't gotta worry about that."

Tyreik eyed her suspiciously then resumed driving. After picking out a 40 inch LCD flatscreen, Chyna returned home. Tyreik helped her bring it in the house.

"India here?" He asked following her up the steps.

"Nah, she at my cousin house."

Once they reached her bedroom, Chyna placed down her purse and eyed him hungrily. Nothing about him had changed. He'd only gotten better with time. His smooth, cocoa skin whispered her name. She longed to feel his muscular arms in the palms of her hands. Her clit yearned for his wet tongue.

At that moment, Chyna came to the conclusion that she was in love with what she would never be able to attain. If she couldn't have all of him, she would gladly take a piece. Tyreik placed the flatscreen down on the floor and stood up straight.

"A'ight, I'm about to head out." He turned around and faced her. "I don't want you to be late for your date."

"Hold up." Chyna placed her hand on his chest. "Stay for a bit."

"Thought you had a date?"

"Really?" Chyna bit her bottom lip seductively. "C'mon, stay."

Tyreik examined her face. He couldn't fall for her big, brown eyes and dimpled cheeks. No matter how sexy she looked or how bad he wanted to fuck her, he had to go. He saw the look of hunger in Chyna's eyes. He wanted no parts of it. Chyna could be very persuasive when she wanted to be.

"Nah, I gotta go, man." He fought his urges.

"Just hear me out." Chyna spoke almost above a whisper. "Tyreik, I miss you and I know you miss me too. You can't tell me you don't." She stepped closer.

Her full breasts were pinned against his chest. She could tell by the look in his eyes that he wanted her just as much as she wanted him. Their sexual chemistry was undeniable. Chyna wanted him in the worst way.

"I need you." She pushed the arms of his jacket down allowing it to fall to the floor.

Chyna wanted nothing more than to bury her nose in his skin. This was what she lived for. When she was with him she came alive. No other human being on the planet had this effect on her. She was addicted to him. She had to have him.

"You're mine." She stood on her tippy toes and kissed his lips sensually.

Before he knew it, Tyreik found himself entrapped in her touch.

"Chyna, stop." He tried to resist but found it hard to.

Chyna's breasts were practically spilling out of her top. She smelled like candy.

"Just give us another chance." She placed a trail of kisses from his lips down to his neck.

"Nah, man, we ain't no good for each other."

"This don't feel good to you?" She caressed the crotch of his jeans.

Tyreik closed his eyes and relished the feel of her stroking his hard dick.

"You gotta chill. I'ma end up fuckin' the shit outta you." He warned.

"I want you to." Chyna purred, dropping to her knees. "You love me just as much as I love you." She said unzipping his pants.

"We owe it to each other to try again." She looked up at him with lustful eyes.

Tyreik stared back at her. He'd never seen a prettier sight than her on her knees. She'd learned her lesson. He would take her back now but only on his terms.

"IF HIS LOVE IS REAL, HE GOTTA HANDLE COMPETITION." —LL COOL J FEAT. BOYZ II MEN, HEY LOVER

CHAPTER 22

"That skirt is cute." Brooke pointed her manicured stiletto nail.

She and Chyna was window shopping down Washington Avenue. They were both casually dressed. Brooke rocked a black, leather, motorcycle jacket, black V-neck tee, black skinny legs with ripped knees and Jordan 3's. Chyna opted for a more military inspired look. She rocked a camo jacket, white tee shirt tied in the front, skin tight jeans and Tims. Her hair was up in a top knot and she wore her favorite pair of gold, door knocker earrings.

"That is cute." She agreed as they continued to walk.

Brooke had her dog, London, with them. He walked ahead of them on a leash. Chyna hated dogs, including Brooke's. London was crazy as hell. He never stopped barking and wouldn't hesitate to bite you. Chyna tried her best to stay clear of him. He was nothing but a Yorkshire Terrier but Chyna didn't care. All dogs in her mind were devil spawn creatures.

"When are we going back inside?" She whined.

Brooke lived in a loft building up the street.

"It's getting cold," Chyna shivered rubbing her arms.

Fall was in full swing. The sun had officially disappeared. The sky was cloudy and gray.

"As soon as he pees we'll go back inside," Brooke replied.

"Huhhhhhh," Chyna groaned. "Don't you got puppy pads in the house?"

"He needed to come outside." Brook rolled her eyes.

"Whatever."

"She always hating on you, London," Brooke made kissy faces at her dog.

Little did Chyna know but she had a secret admirer. From across the way, Carlos got out of his silver Mercedes-AMG GT S. He'd noticed her as soon as he pulled on the block. Chyna was bad. How could he forget her? She looked like the type of chick you wife'd. Babygirl was fly. He wanted to give her keys to the whip.

She'd been on his mind since he'd seen her at the restaurant. He'd hoped for months that he'd get the chance to see her again. Now here she was live in the flesh. She was no longer a figment of his imagination. Carlos dug everything about her. Her around the way, b-girl inspired look was totally different from the revealing dress she wore the last time he saw her.

From the far away look in her eyes, he could tell she still had a man. None of that mattered. He didn't give a damn. She was meant to be with him. She would one day bear his last name. Carlos gave dap to his homeboys then they proceeded up the street in her direction. Brooke peeped them immediately. She could smell money from a mile away.

"Uh oh, fine nigga alert. How I look?" She asked running her hand down the back of her head.

"You cute!" Chyna checked her face then spotted the group of guys.

It was as if time slowed. Something in the universe directed her to Carlos. Out of the group of dudes, her eyes landed on him. His face seemed familiar but she couldn't pin point where she knew him from. All she knew was that the only white boy out the click was gorgeous. She'd never seen anything like him.

The dude was that deal. On sight he could get it. She didn't know who he was but he looked at her as if he could see into her soul. She was vulnerable under his gaze. Dude was tall, just how she liked 'em. He looked to be about 6'1. He had slicked-back, black hair. His sides were tapered and shaved low. His thick brows furrowed above his hazel, diamond-cut eyes.

A five o'clock beard covered his modelesque face. Chyna found herself wanting to kiss his lips. She was entranced by him. Visions of them making love under the moonlight filled her mind. Although it was a squad of them, he stood out the most. He led the pack of dudes with confidence.

He donned a black, Balmain, letterman's jacket with black, leather sleeves, a black tee, black, fitted, Rag & Bone jeans and black Tims. A simple gold Rolex watch adorned his wrist. He didn't need to do much to look good. His mere being was beautiful. Chyna cleared her throat and pushed her boobs out as he approached.

"You can stop stalkin' me now." Carlos extended his tattooed hand.

"Excuse you?" Chyna smiled shyly, taken aback by his forwardness.

"Don't act like you ain't been eye-fuckin' me since I walked up the street," Carlos smiled.

"What?" Chyna said at a lost for words.

Carlos immediately had her on her toes.

"I'm just fuckin' wit' you. What's your name, sweetheart?"

"Chyna." She shook his hand nervously.

"You can call me Los. Here," he used his free hand to hand her his phone. "Give me your number."

"Excuse you?" Chyna cocked her head back.

"Don't act like you don't want to," he challenged.

"I don't even know you and plus, I gotta man." Chyna remembered Tyreik.

They weren't back together but they were working on things. She didn't want to do anything that would jeopardize that.

"Normally, I would respect that and keep it moving but I don't give a fuck about ya' man. I can tell you ain't happy."

"Bruh, you don't even know me," Chyna laughed awestruck by him.

"I ain't gotta know you to know that. The fact that you're still holding my hand tells me everything I need to know." He grinned seductively.

Chyna looked down at her hand intertwined with his and quickly pulled it away.

"I'ma make it easy on you. Let me see your phone," Carlos held out his hand.

"No!" Chyna took a step back.

"Why you frontin'? You know you want to."

Chyna inhaled deep. *This dude gotta lot of nerve,* she thought. He was cocky as hell. She liked an aggressive man. Plus, he was sexy as hell. She and Tyreik weren't technically together. It wouldn't be like she was cheating if she took his number. She could have friends. Chyna reached inside her jacket pocket and handed Carlos her phone. He added his number to her contacts.

"Don't wait too long to call me." He handed her back her phone.

"You betta get yo' life. I'm not callin' you," Chyna blushed.

"Yes you are." Carlos winked his eye before walking off.

"What the fuck was that?" Brooke clutched a set of invisible pearls.

"I don't know... but I think I'm pregnant," Chyna fanned herself.

"IF HE CAN FUCK YOU, HE CAN HELP YOU. IF HE CAN'T HELP YOU, THEN WHY YOU FUCKIN' HIM?" —SOURCE UNKNOWN

CHAPTER 23

"I don't want no relations...I just want yo' facials...Girl, you know you like a pistol...You a throw away. " Future's Throw Away bumped through the speakers of Tyreik's truck. Chyna bobbed her head to the beat. They were heading to dinner. She felt like the boss she was whenever she was by his side. Trap music and Tyreik always equaled a good time. They both looked good and smelled even better. Tyreik stayed fresh to death.

His new job at GM was doing the boy good. Chyna peeped his Lanvin, quilted bomber jacket, Alexander Wang, neoprene tee shirt, Citizens of Humanity jeans and Lebron James sneakers. It didn't go over her head that since he started working he hadn't kicked her down any dough. Sure, he was taking her to dinner that night but a meal didn't compare to feeding, clothing and housing a nigga.

He could've at least given her a couple hundred just to say thank you. Chyna's thank you however was on his back. Making a mental note, she pulled out her Chanel compact mirror. She had to make sure she was on point. She looked at herself in the mirror. Her face was on fleek but no amount of makeup could hide the fact that Tyreik had managed to turn her from a woman of substance to an object to play with. She never intended to be this chick. But here she was settling for any, old thing just to stake some kind of claim on a man that was never really hers.

"Fuck!" Tyreik hit his hand on the steering wheel.

"What's wrong wit' you?" Chyna looked at him like he was crazy.

"I left my I.D. at the crib. I'ma have to swing by there real quick."

Chyna pursed her lips together. Whenever he brought up his apartment she couldn't help but feel some type of way. A) It fucked her up that he could pay rent some place else but he couldn't when he was staying with her. B) She didn't like Tyreik having his own spot. She was always paranoid that when she wasn't in contact with him that he'd have another chick there. It wasn't like Chyna had a car to do drive-bys in. C) This was her first time ever going to his spot. He hadn't invited her over once.

She was starting to think that he didn't want her to know where she stayed. Shortly after, he pulled onto a secluded street on the Southside. Tyreik parked in front of a newly remodeled 4 family flat.

"I'll be right back. You coming in?" He placed one foot out the door.

"Oh, you inviting me in?" Chyna placed her hand on her chest shocked.

"Man, get out," Tyreik chuckled.

Chyna stepped out and followed him up the walkway. She looked around and made a mental note of the street name as he unlocked the door. After walking up a flight of stairs, they made their way onto the main floor of the apartment. Chyna was pleasantly surprised. Tyreik's crib was nice. He had hardwood floors, stainless steel appliances, a wash room and balcony. It was just enough room for him. There was hardly any furniture in there. All he had was a couch, coffee table, king size bed and a 50 inch flatscreen television.

"Oh, so you can buy you a TV but you couldn't replace mine? Oh ok?" She nodded.

"Don't start." Tyreik scowled, while rummaging through a pile of dirty clothes that was on the floor.

"I'ma be outside while you look for your I.D." Chyna crossed her arms across her chest.

"You really call yo'self having an attitude?" He stopped what he was doing and glared at her.

"Yep." Chyna walked carefully down the stairs.

She had on six inch heels. Back in the car she sat fuming. *What the fuck am I doing? This nigga is the worst. He don't give a fuck about me.* She halfway wanted to tell him to take her home. The only thing stopping her was the hunger pangs in her stomach. Chyna could tolerate him for a few hours in order to eat. Tyreik locked his door and jogged over to the car. Chyna watched him with disdain. Freezing, he jumped back inside the truck.

"I found it." He held up his I.D.

"Good for you." Chyna shot sarcastically staring out the window.

She didn't give a damn about him or his I.D.

"You are such a fuckin' brat." He grabbed her face and made her kiss him.

With each flicker of his tongue Chyna became lost. She hated that he could have her on the verge of insanity one minute then longing for his touch the next. Tyreik gave her one last peck before pulling away.

"You done poutin'?" He started the ignition.

"Yeah," she grinned like an innocent school girl.

"SO WHEN HE GOES OUT TO THE CLUB WITH THE BOYS, I'MA HIT YOU UP." —MONICA, HERE I AM

CHAPTER 24

The scene was set. The lights were dimmed low, SiR played softly, candles were lit and a bottle of Dom was being chilled. Massage oils were on display and Chyna wore the sexiest piece of lingerie she owned. Her inner vixen was on full display. A black, Chantilly, lace bralette cupped her voluptuous, caramel breasts. A matching thong and leather suspender set accentuated her round ass and succulent thighs.

The leather straps from the suspenders hugged her thighs and highlighted the black, Louboutin *Pigalle* heels she wore on her feet. She wore her hair wild and curly just the way Tyreik liked it. Homegirl was feeling herself. She'd been planning a night of seduction all week. India was gone to her mother's so she and Tyreik could get as freaky as they wanted to be. Chyna detested having to dial back her freak meter.

She liked to be as uninhibited and loud as the mood called for. Standing in the center of the bedroom, she checked the time on her watch. It was past 8:00pm. Tyreik was supposed to be there by 7:00pm. She didn't want to hound him but Chyna was impatient. She hated when people were late. It bugged the hell out of her. Tyreik hadn't even picked up the phone to tell her why he was M.I.A. Becoming irritated, she located her phone and called him. Chyna fanned herself as the phone rang. It had started to become hot because of the candles.

"Hello?" He answered with a laugh.

Chyna immediately zeroed in on the loud chatter in the background. He wasn't on the way at all.

"Where you at?"

"I'm still at the crib, babe. Kingston and Rob stopped by. We in here choppin' it up."

"You know I'm over here waiting on you, right? I got something special planned."

"I'm coming. Just give me a minute. I'll be there in an hour," Tyreik said tenderly.

"A'ight," Chyna sighed heavily.

"Aye?"

"What?" Chyna replied with an attitude.

"Fix yo' face. I'm coming," Tyreik promised.

"I could be cumming if yo' ass would hurry up," she spat.

"Shut up. I'll call you when I'm on my way," Tyreik laughed some.

"Ok." Chyna giggled, ending the call.

An hour and forty five minutes later, Tyreik was still nowhere to be found. Chyna lie on her bed beyond annoyed. She was incensed. *This nigga has no regard for me or my time,* she thought. The candles were damn near about to die out, they'd been burning so long. The ice that kept the champagne chilled had melted. Chyna was one more yawn away from falling asleep.

Rolling over, she called Tyreik. To her displeasure he didn't answer. Her blood immediately started to boil. *Not this shit again.* On edge, she called him several times. He didn't answer either call. *Ok, I'ma call one more time and if he don't answer then fuck it,* she told herself. The fourth time must've been her lucky charm because he answered. Relieved, Chyna exhaled a sigh of relief.

"What's up, babe?"

"Ok, this is ridiculous. Where are you at?" She snapped unable to control her anger.

"I swear to God, I'm coming," Tyreik laughed.

Chyna rolled her eyes to the sky. She could tell he was drunk.

"When? It's already been damn near three hours!"

"Yo, chill. I said I was coming," Tyreik said becoming irritated by her line of questioning. "I'm in the car right now," he lied.

"For real?" Chyna got her hopes up.

"Yeah."

"Stop lyin', nigga! You act like she gon' beat yo' ass or something!" Kingston taunted him in the background.

"You still at home?!" Chyna shrieked.

"I thought I told yo' ass to be quiet," Tyreik laughed.

"Tyreik!" Chyna shouted, jumping out of bed. "Please tell me you are not still at home!"

"I'm still here," he admitted. "We drinkin' and talkin' shit."

"Yo' ass ain't coming," Chyna responded disappointed.

She was so mad she could spit.

"To be honest wit' you, I think I'ma chill here tonight," Tyreik confessed.

Chyna screwed up her face.

"If you felt that way, you could'a said that three hours ago instead of having me sitting here waiting on you!"

"I changed my mind," he replied nonchalantly.

"Yo…you are a piece of work." Chyna looked around the room at the romantic night she'd planned.

All of it had become a complete waste of time.

"I don't know why I continue to do this shit wit' you. You don't give a fuck about nobody but yourself. You knew I had this shit planned all week long."

"Yo, I don't know what you on but you need to fall back. We ain't together. I don't owe you shit. I'm sorry that whatever you had planned got fucked up but that's on you. I ain't tell you to do that shit. You did that shit on yo' own. If I don't wanna come, I'm not gon' come. Period!"

Chyna held the phone speechless. It was bad enough that he had the nerve to disrespect her but it was worse that he had the nerve to do it in front of his friends.

"I'm not about to let you ruin my night 'cause you wanna be mad. Shit, you always fuckin' mad. Go find something to do that'll make yo' ass happy. 'Cause you gettin' on my fuckin' nerves! I don't know who you think I am. But I'm not about to kiss yo' ass."

"Who are you talkin' to?" Chyna felt another crack being etched into her heart.

"I'm talkin' to you!" Tyreik exclaimed. "Man, fuck this. I'll holla at you later." He hung up in her ear.

Paralyzed by his utter lack of empathy, Chyna fell into a heap on the floor. She was coming undone. *Why do you continue to let him do this to you,* she asked herself. A stream of tears danced in her eyes. For once she wished he could feel how he made her feel. Was he blind to the pain he was causing inside of her? She never broke one promise to him.

She always kept her word. There was never a time where she wasn't there for him. She could never depend on him. Chyna was always left to fend for herself. She always had to pick herself up and put herself back together again. She wanted to walk in his shoes and see how it felt to live so selfishly. She wished she could make him hurt.

She was sick of being the one always left alone to cry. She was tired of dating herself. It was apparent that what they shared was a one-sided affair. Tyreik treated her like an ugly stepchild and her dumb-ass kept running back for more. He didn't respect her. Chyna didn't give him a reason to. She was his doormat. He knew how much she loved him and played off her emotions.

He knew she'd always forgive him. Realizing she was attending a party for one, Chyna tearfully reached for the bottle of Dom. She didn't even bother getting a glass. Homegirl drank straight from the bottle. She took it straight to the head. Getting a glimpse of herself in the mirror, she admired how good she looked. Chyna slid her hand across her breasts. The fabric felt good on her skin.

She needed to feel wanted. Somebody had to care about her well-being. Hell, what Tyreik didn't want, another man would gladly appreciate. Chyna took another big gulp from the bottle and wiped her mouth with the back of her hand. All she wanted was to love and be loved. On her knees, she crawled over to her phone and went through her contacts. Carlos' name stared back at her. She contemplated on whether or not she should call. It had been weeks since they met. He probably wouldn't even remember who she was.

"Fuck it." She said deciding to hit him up.

She would be damned if she let the night be a total waste.

"Took you long enough," he answered after the third ring.

"How you know it's me?" Chyna asked, tipsy.

"I took a wild guess," Carlos admitted.

The deep bass in his voice sent chills up Chyna's spine.

"Oh," she laughed. "What you doing?"

"Why? You wanna see me?"

"As a matter-of-fact, I do."

"Give me your address. I'm on my way."

"TIME STANDS STILL WHENEVER YOU'RE NEAR ME." —KEKE WYATT, LIE UNDER YOU

CHAPTER 25

Chyna got rid of any evidence of a sexy night's rendezvous and quickly changed her clothes. It was already bad enough she had a man she barely knew coming to her house during the middle of the night. Thinking on her feet, she texted Brooke.

<Messages **Brooke** Details

In case I come up dead... The white boy on his way over here

Brooke immediately responded back.

<Messages **Brooke** Details

Bitch, what?!!!!!!!!! 'Bout time! Don't get nothin' on ya!!!

Nearly an hour later, Carlos knocked on her door. Chyna did a quick check in the mirror to make sure her hair and makeup were still straight. It was. Pleased with herself, she unlocked the door. Carlos gazed down at her. She was still as beautiful as he remembered. The only thing different was her hair. The last time her hair was straight and in a bun. Now her hair was filled with bountiful curls that framed her angelic face perfectly.

She was casually dressed in an oversized, Celine tee shirt, cut-off jeans and leopard print, moccasin, house shoes. He loved the fact that she didn't try to do too much to impress him. Chyna didn't have to. In Carlos' eyes she was perfect just the way she was.

Chyna was at a loss for words. Carlos was the truth. She was mesmerized by him. His presence commanded her attention. Like her, he was laid back with his look. His hair was slicked back giving him a James Dean, 1950's sex appeal. He donned a red and black, lumber jack button up, a denim blue jean jacket, jeans and rust colored Tims. The cold weather caused the tip of his nose to turn red. Chyna wanted to make love to his face.

"You gon' let me in or nah?" He smirked.

Chyna blinked her eyes and came back to reality.

"Yeah," she stepped to the side.

Carlos walked past her with a large, brown bag and a blanket in tow.

"What's that?" Chyna quizzed leading him to the second floor of the house.

"Sushi, I figured you might be hungry."

"You tryin' to call me fat?" Chyna joked.

"Nah," Carlos cracked up laughing.

"Well, I'm just letting you know right now, I'm not fuckin' you," Chyna declared as they walked into the kitchen.

"Yes you are." Carlos stated confidently placing the food on the kitchen counter. "But why you say that?"

"'Cause if you feed me, I will fuck you."

"You silly." He shook his head enjoying her witty banter. "I also bought a bottle of wine."

"Oh yeah, you gettin' some tonight." Chyna pretended to faint.

"You like white or red?" Carlos removed his jacket.

"White, obviously." Chyna looked him up and down.

"You wild." Carlos pulled a pistol from out of the back of his jeans.

"Jesus, be a fence! He about to kill me!" Chyna flinched terrified. "I knew I shouldn't have called yo' white ass over here! All you crackers are crazy!" She ran and hid in the corner.

"Are you done?" Carlos looked at her as if she were insane.

Chyna peeked out at him.

"You not gon' kill me?" She whispered.

"No, I like my freedom. I'm licensed to carry, sweetheart. You said you had a man, remember? For all I know, he could be crazy. I ain't tryin' to let nobody run up on me."

"Oh." Chyna came from out of the corner. "You ain't gotta worry about that. He ain't coming over here."

Tyreik was doing him. Chyna was the last thing on his mind and she knew it.

"You don't remember me, do you?" Carlos asked as she came back into the kitchen.

"What you mean?" Chyna replied confused.

"I saw you back in January at Mango. You almost fell. I caught you." He jogged her memory.

"OH MY GOD! That was you?" Chyna shrieked, playfully pushing his arm.

"Yeah."

"I thought I knew you from somewhere."

"Yeah, I've had my eye on you for a long time," Carlos confessed.

"Is that right?" Chyna twirled one of her curls around her finger.

It took everything in Carlos not to take her right then and there on the kitchen floor.

"You ready to eat?" He asked trying his best not to rip off her clothes.

"Yeah."

"Cool, grab some plates, please."

Chyna found it refreshing to have a man take control. With Tyreik she was always the leader. A woman liked to be led and taken care of. Carlos was already winning brownie points for being attentive. Chyna took out two plates.

"Hand me those," he requested.

Perplexed, she handed him the plates.

"What you got planned?"

"I got this. Let me take care of you. The only thing I want you to do is turn on some music."

Chyna happily did as she was asked. She ran up to her bedroom and retrieved her tablet. She turned it on as she walked back down the steps. Her SoundCloud playlist was the shit. She had music from Alex Isley, Lana Del Rey and Justine Skye. She was sure he'd like her song choices. By the time she made it back to the second floor, Carlos had a whole picnic scene set up.

He'd moved her coffee table to the side. In the center of the floor was now the blanket he brought, the bottle of wine, two wine glasses, two sets of chopsticks and napkins. The plates were filled with a variety of sushi. He sat awaiting her return looking like a Greek god.

"Oh my God. You did not have to do all of this," Chyna gushed, feeling like a princess.

"You good. Sit down." Carlos smiled pleased to see she was ecstatic.

Chyna sat Indian style beside him. She didn't want to sit across from him. She wanted to be near him and feel his energy.

"Thank you for this." She nudged him on the arm with her shoulder. "I had a really tough night," she admitted sadly.

"I can tell you've been crying." Carlos poured her a glass of wine.

"How you figure that?" Chyna drew her head back.

"'Cause you're eyes are still red." He pointed out.

Chyna rolled her eyes. It slightly annoyed her that he paid so much attention to her. She wanted to be some sort of mystery to him.

"Stop…," she paused unable to gather her thoughts. "Get out of my business!" She burst out laughing.

"Don't get mad at me. I ain't the one that made you cry." He handed her glass to her.

"But you are the one making me smile," Chyna smiled warmly.

Over the course of the next few hours, she and Carlos talked about everything from love to religion. Nothing was off limits. He made her feel free to express herself. He didn't pass judgment on anything she had to say. Chyna found him to be brilliant and charming. He had a dry sense of humor that she couldn't get enough of. She'd almost forgotten how it felt to laugh with someone. By the time the sun started to rise, they were still awake. They lie side-by-side on top of the blanket. A soft hue of gray light cascaded over their bodies.

"What's your favorite color?" She whispered.

"Black."

"I should've known that," she joked.

"You're ridiculous," Carlos grinned enjoying her company. "Yours are black and pink, right?" He quizzed.

"How you know?" Chyna gasped astonished.

"You got it all over your damn house."

"Oh, yeah." She giggled feeling dumb.

"Favorite place you've ever visited?" Carlos questioned, playing with her hand.

He'd fallen in love with her delicate fingers.

"Miami." Chyna blushed, taking pleasure in his soft touch.

"Mines is Bali. It was beautiful there."

"I can imagine. I've never been out of the country. I've been everywhere in the U.S. but never across the pond," Chyna admitted.

"We gon' have to change that. That's no bueno," Carlos replied.

"Best book you've ever read?" Chyna turned over and faced him.

"George R.R. Martin's Game of Thrones series. You watch the show?" Carlos looked at her.

"Uh, yeah," Chyna replied excited. "It's like, one of my favorite shows of all time."

"Who's your favorite character?"

"Daenerys and Tyrion," Chyna said quickly.

It was refreshing to talk to someone about things other than Love and Hip Hop. She'd tried to get Tyreik to take interest in the show but since it wasn't ratchet he couldn't relate.

"Tyrion is my boy but I like Jon Snow too."

"Me too."

"I can't believe you watch Game of Thrones," Carlos said delightfully thrilled.

"Why, 'cause I'm black?" Chyna teased, squinting her eyes.

"No, 'cause most pretty girls like you don't like gruesome, period shows," Carlos corrected her.

"I'm not like most girls," Chyna verified.

"I see." Carlos licked his bottom lip.

Chyna felt her clit jump.

"Guiltiest pleasure?"

"Ok…you're going to think I'm disgusting but I love Doritos and oysters," Chyna said cautiously.

"Together?" Carlos replied shocked.

Chyna nodded her head.

"Yeah, that's fuckin' disgusting," he grinned.

"It's delicious, I'm tellin' you."

"I'll take your word for it."

"How about you?" Chyna died to know

"Kissing you," Carlos said in a low, raspy tone.

His speaking voice reminded her of the rapper Nas.

"But you haven't kissed me yet," Chyna tried to steady her breathing.

Excitement was stirring inside her.

"I could be a terrible kisser for all you know," she whispered.

"Never." Carlos leaned over and placed his lips upon hers.

Under the watchful gaze of the sun, Carlos and Chyna shared their first kiss. Chyna's kisses were slow and succulent, just like he'd imagined. He wanted to devour every ounce of her. But Carlos vowed to take his time with Chyna. He could tell she was fragile. She needed time to heal her *Paper Heart*. When she gave herself to him he wanted her to give him her all. He wouldn't accept anything less.

"I'LL BE DAMN IF I GIVE YOU MY LOVE AND YOU DO ME THE SAME."
—JENNI LOVETTE, PAPER HEART

CHAPTER 26

A week had gone by without any communication between Chyna and Tyreik. For once she didn't mind. It was actually peaceful without having him around. Chyna was on such a high from her night with Carlos that she didn't miss Tyreik at all. In one night, Carlos showed her that there didn't have to be a constant battle between a woman and a man. Everything with him was easy.

She couldn't get him off her mind. He'd permanently taken up space there. They talked everyday. She found herself giddy with expectation each time he called. It had been years since she felt butterflies. The fact that she hadn't talked to Tyreik was a second thought. Normally, she would've blown up his phone, begging him to speak to her, but not this time.

Chyna was getting her swag back. She still loved him but she was done sweating Tyreik. It was time she put his ass on ice. It was high time she made him wonder what she was doing and who she was with. At the laundromat she pulled her and India's things out of the washer. Miss Charlene, the laundromat supervisor, was cussing out a white customer as usual.

It was her forte. Miss Charlene would cuss yo' ass out in a heartbeat, especially if you interrupted her phone call. The whole time she worked she stayed gossiping on the phone with her best friend Shirley. It was fairly empty in the laundromat. Chyna wouldn't have a problem getting one of the dryers. Humming along to Beyoncé's smash hit, *Drunk In Love,* she rolled her cart of wet clothes to the dryer section. Chyna had the album on repeat. She was a die-hard Beyoncé fan.

She literally lost her mind when the secret album dropped. *Mine* and *No Angel* were some of her favorite standout tracks. Chyna was in the middle of loading her last dryer when a call came in and interrupted her Beyoncé jam session. She hoped it was Carlos calling. She hadn't talked to him all day. From the ringtone, she knew it wasn't. It was Tyreik.

Disappointed, she frowned and contemplated whether or not to answer. The only reason he was hitting her up was because it was his birthday. Half the day had gone by and Chyna hadn't reached out to him once. She knew he had to be stunned. This was the first time she wasn't on her knees begging to be in his presence. Chyna quite enjoyed the new-found confidence she'd gained but by the fifth ring she picked up the line.

"Yeah," she said dryly.

"How you doing, miss lady?" Tyreik said nicely.

Chyna took the phone away from her ear to make sure she was speaking to the right person.

"Who is this? 'Cause it can't be Tyreik!" She remarked mockingly.

"You know damn well it's me."

"What you want? Last time I talked to you, you cussed me out and hung up on me." Chyna quipped starting the dryer.

"'Cause you was trippin'." Tyreik responded honestly.

"It's always myfault.com. Are you ever gon' take responsibility for the shit you do?"

"Look, I was wrong for hanging up on you. That was wrong. I just needed a minute to breathe, to do me."

"You must've needed a lot of air 'cause it's been a whole week," Chyna shot.

"I figured I'd give us a minute," Tyreik reasoned.

"My minute ain't up yet 'cause I'm still mad." Chyna sat on a wooden bench by the candy dispenser. "You ain't gon' keep talkin' to me crazy and think that shit is ok."

"You right and I'ma stop doing that. You gotta admit though, it is kinda fucked up that you haven't called to wish me a happy birthday. I thought me and you was better than that?"

"Why would I? We ain't together, remember?" Chyna said with a sudden fierceness.

"I knew you was gon' say that," Tyreik laughed quietly. "You already know what it is between me and you. You gon' be my baby forever."

"Spit that game, boy!" Chyna snapped her fingers.

"You know that ain't even me. I don't spit game. I do miss you tho'."

"Is that right?" Chyna crossed her legs.

"Yeah, I wanna come through. If that's a'ight wit' you?"

"For what?" Chyna grimaced.

"I wanna spend my birthday wit' you. I was thinkin' we could order some pizza and me, you and India play Monopoly like we used to." Tyreik hoped she'd say yes.

"Who paying?" Chyna retorted.

"Me, nigga!" Tyreik shouted offended.

Chyna giggled. Tyreik always knew how to tug on her heartstrings. When things were good with them, they'd often have fun at home like that. They were all truly happy on nights like those. Moments like that is what made her love Tyreik. He knew how to be a family man when he wanted to be.

"I don't know if that's a good idea," Chyna said unwilling to give in.

"Since when seeing me ain't a good idea? C'mon, it's my birthday. I wanna see you," Tyreik said coyly.

Low key, apart of Chyna wanted to see him too. But then she remembered all the drama that came along with him.

"This past week has been hella peaceful. I'm not tryin' to go backwards."

"Me either. The last thing I wanna do is fight with you. I ain't tryin' to hurt you. You gon' be my wife one day. Hell, maybe sooner than you think," Tyreik threw in for good measure.

Chyna had totally forgotten about her marriage ultimatum. The end of 2013 was near. She couldn't believe that Tyreik had remembered and was taking her seriously. The thought of him finally making good on his promise and putting a ring on it made her feel like all of her hard work was finally paying off. Maybe all the turmoil she'd been through with him hadn't been a total waste of time.

Maybe she could still have her happily ever after. Maybe their short stint apart had pumped some fear in his heart. Maybe he'd finally seen that she wasn't replaceable. Maybe he realized it was time for him to change. Chyna could beat the curse on her family and become the first woman to be married. She'd be able to show her mother,

India, Brooke and Asia that beneath all the rubble, Tyreik really did love her.

"I just wanna be wit' you and India. I don't wanna be nowhere else," Tyreik said sincerely.

"Ok." Chyna replied softly, giving in.

"I'M STILL A CANINE AT HEART, I'MA DOG."

-DRAKE FEAT. TRAVIS SCOTT, COMPANY

CHAPTER 27

Chyna and Tyreik stayed into it but that was the dynamic of their relationship. They loved hard and fought even harder. On New Year's Day 2014 nothing had changed. They had a tumultuous night. Tyreik being the flashy, charismatic man he was, decided to buy the bar out at the Delmar Lounge.

Chyna was already in a bad mood because the holidays had come and gone and she still hadn't received a ring. Once again, she'd taken a bite out of the rotten apple and almost lost her life. She was so sick of him selling her a dream. She'd completely pushed Carlos away because she thought she had a ring on the way. On top of that, Tyreik had barely said a word to her all night.

Chyna sat back with her legs crossed seething in anger as he strolled around the bar unbothered by her attitude. Tyreik was having a good ole time. He had the spot going crazy. He was drinking, dancing and mingling as if he didn't have a care in the world. Chick after chick came up to speak to him. Chyna hated that he was even entertaining them hoes. She knew he was only doing it to piss her off and it was working.

She tried to play it cool because she was with Brooke. Everybody knew Chyna was a hothead but she didn't wanna come across as the jealous and insecure type anymore. Her friend didn't need to know that she and Tyreik were still having problems. Chyna sat with her legs and arms crossed watching his every move. She couldn't take her eyes off of him. Tyreik knew how to control a room. He was a lady-killer.

Chyna watched closely as a chick with thick, red, wavy weave approached him. The broad looked just like a girl she'd caught him with two years prior. Chyna hadn't even told her friends about the situation. She was too embarrassed. The incident happened during the time Tyreik moved out the first time. Chyna instantly flashed back to the day

It was a typical Saturday. She lived in North County then. Chyna woke up ready to start her day. She and Tyreik were going through a rough time, like always. For the one zillionth time they were trying to repair their relationship. Chyna was doing her best to adjust to him living alone. The process hadn't been easy. Tyreik made it difficult for her too. Wanting to say hi, she texted him:

<Messages **Tyreik** Details

Morning, baby

She didn't think anything of it when he didn't respond right back but after an hour she started to wonder what was up. Instead of texting him, this time she called. She didn't get any response. Figuring he was busy, she went on about her day. After a few hours passed without any contact from him she began to worry.

Chyna called him again to no avail. Her body instantly tensed up. The old, familiar feeling of Tyreik being up to no good was creeping back. Before she knew it, Chyna found herself locked in her bedroom calling him back-to-back. She couldn't focus on anything else. Each time the phone rang and he didn't pick up pushed her further and further down the rabbit hole of denial.

By nightfall, she'd called him over a hundred times. Needing answers to why he wasn't answering her calls, Chyna came up with the genius idea to catch a cab to his place. It was after midnight. She'd left India at home alone and told her not to open the door for anyone. Chyna knew she was being an absolute, out of control, psycho idiot but all of that went out of the window as she took a $30 cab ride to South City.

If Tyreik was on some bullshit she was going to find out. However, when she made it to his place, his car wasn't there. Not satisfied with her findings, she had the cab driver swing by Kingston's place. If he wasn't at home he might've been there. Unfortunately for Chyna, his car wasn't there either. Chyna was still as clueless as before to why he wasn't answering her calls. Why would he wake up and decide to ignore her calls?

The roundtrip ride ended up costing her a cool $60 but Chyna didn't give a fuck. She was on a mission. The first thing she did when she got back home was check on India. She was safe and sound in her room watching television. On the verge of having a mental breakdown, she resumed blowing up Tyreik's phone. Hot tears scorched her face. The tears wouldn't stop flowing as his voicemail continuously clicked in.

"Why is he doing this to me?" She paced back and forth madly. "I didn't even do anything to him. Like, why?"

For the next five hours, Chyna texted and called him until her fingers became sore. She'd become a crazed animal. She cried so much her eyes had begun to sting. It was now 7:00am. Figuring he'd be home by now, she called another cab. The sun was out and shining brightly. India was sound asleep in her room. Just in case she woke up while she was gone, Chyna wrote a quick note telling her she'd be right back.

To her surprise, Chyna got the same cab driver as before. Once again she had him drive by Tyreik's crib. A since of dread washed over her when she pulled up to his building and saw his car wasn't there. Her worst fears were coming true. He was with another girl. There was no other explanation. Chyna was about to head back home when something told her to go back by Kingston's spot.

Chyna held her breath as the cab neared his apartment building. A sense of relief filled her heart when she pulled up and saw Tyreik's car outside. *Ok, maybe they went out. He got drunk and spent the night,* she thought calming down some. Her heart told her to accept the fact that he was there but her mind told her to push further for the truth.

"I'll be right back." Chyna told the cab driver as she got out.

The meter was running. She'd already spent over $30 again and still had to return home. Chyna didn't give a fuck about the money. She needed to know why. With the determination of a woman scorned, she stormed inside the building. She'd never been inside the building so she didn't know where Kingston's apartment was. Using her street smarts, she looked at the names on the mailboxes. It didn't take long to locate Kingston's apartment.

He stayed in apartment 3B. Chyna took the steps two at a time until she reached his door. Out of breath because she'd decided to wear heels, Chyna caught her breath. If she was going to be on crazy bitch status, she was going to look good while doing it. Kingston's door was wooden and had a small window. A gray curtain covered it but she could see through the thin fabric.

Before knocking, she stood on her tip toes and peeked inside. She could see a small part of the living room. Terror shocked her to the core when she looked down. She spotted two sets of feet. A woman's and a man's feet were resting on the arm of the couch. Chyna wanted to scream. She knew every limb on Tyreik's body. It was implanted in her brain. Those were his damn feet she was staring at.

At that point, Chyna Danae Black, the best-selling author and doting mother of one was no longer there. That chick had officially left the building and traveled to outer space. Crazy had reared its ugly head. Chyna raised her fist and bammed on the door. It took a second but Kingston came to the door. She saw him coming from the back of the apartment. He didn't have a shirt on. Chyna stepped back as he opened the door. Groggily, Kingston rubbed his eyes.

"What's up?" He said hoarsely.

"Is Tyreik here?" Chyna asked outraged.

Kingston tried his hardest to wake up so he could understand what was going on. He was so sleepy that he couldn't grasp the situation.

"What?" He eyed her curiously.

"I know Tyreik is here! His car is outside! Tell him I'm here!" Chyna demanded.

Her entire body was shaking wildly.

"Hold up." Kingston closed the door in her face.

Chyna stood as patient as she could as she waited for Tyreik to come to the door. Five minutes later, she was still standing there waiting. Chyna snapped and pounded her hand and foot against the door.

"Open the damn door!" She yelled.

She didn't give a fuck about Kingston's neighbors or that it was after 7:00am. They weren't about to play her like she wasn't shit. Chyna would fuck up Tyreik and Kingston too. Since no one had come to the door, she peeked back through the window and saw a girl with long, wavy, red weave placing on her bra.

It took all of the will power Chyna had to swallow the vomit in her throat. She'd physically and mentally had enough. It was apparent that Tyreik wasn't going to come to the door. Chyna had to leave. She had to get out of there before she went to jail. She'd totally forgotten that she was in a cab and that the meter was running. Spent, she walked down the three flights of stairs and headed outside. As she walked to the cab with tears stinging her eyes, Tyreik came from around the back of the building.

"Chyna!" He called out. "What the fuck is yo' problem? What are you doing here?"

"Fuck you, nigga!" Chyna spun around on her heels. "I saw you on the couch with that bitch!"

"What are you talkin' about? I was in that back sleep! That was him on the couch!"

Chyna knew he was lying because she'd seen Kingston walk from the back of the apartment. Unless him and Kingston was fuckin', that nigga was lying.

"Stop lyin'! I know it was you! That's why you ain't been answering my calls 'cause you was wit' another bitch! It's cool tho! Fuck you!" She pointed her finger at him like a gun.

"You wanna disregard me and my feelings?" She raised her right leg and kicked his car repeatedly with her heel.

"I hate yo' ass! I wish you would die!" She kicked the passenger side with all of her might.

"You wish I would die?" Tyreik replied visibly hurt. "That's some fucked-up-ass shit to say, Chyna. It's all good. Remember that shit." He nodded his head.

Without uttering another word, he went back inside the building and left her standing there. Over $120 later,

Chyna returned home felling like a broken porcelain doll. Now here she was two years later in the same position. The girl with the ghetto, red, wavy weave was back. She didn't give him a friendly, one arm hug. She wrapped her arms around his neck and stared longingly in his eyes.

When Tyreik released his arms from around her waist, she kept her arms wrapped around him. On the outside looking in, it looked as if they were messing around. Why Tyreik hadn't removed her arms from around his neck was beyond her. Chyna didn't understand it. Well, what he wouldn't do she would. She wasn't about to be humiliated in front of her friend, his pot'nahs and everyone else that knew them.

Chyna didn't think twice. She rose to her feet and stormed through the crowd. Tyreik didn't even see her coming. Before he knew it, Chyna had placed her hand under his arm and yanked him back.

"Have you lost your fuckin' mind?" She ice grilled him.

"What?" Tyreik chuckled drunkenly.

"Don't fuckin' play wit' me. I will tear this muthafucka up," Chyna warned.

Shocked by the display before her, the girl with the red, wavy weave swiftly scurried away. She didn't want any parts of the crazy look in Chyna's eyes.

"What the fuck is your problem? This what we do now?" She snapped.

"Chill out." Tyreik waved her off. "She was just sayin' hi." He flashed her a devilish grin.

"Ok," Chyna nodded her head. "Think it's a game." She licked her bottom lip fed up.

Pissed that he was trying to act as if he hadn't just disrespected her, Chyna stormed away. She grabbed her Dior bag and signaled to Brooke that it was time to go. Tyreik had her all the way fucked up if he thought she was gonna sit idly by and be played out. She had something for his ass. The Delmar was about to close. It was time to hit up another spot. Chyna turned her phone off and hit up The Boom-Boom Room.

The Boom-Boom Room was as hood as a club could get. The floors weren't finished and there was hardly any décor but the drinks were good and it stayed open till six in the morning. A club staying open till six in morning in St. Louis was illegal but that was the least of Chyna's worries. She was trying to get lit. She ordered herself a stiff drink and danced until her legs became sore.

By the time they left, it was 5am. When she turned her phone back on she had six voicemail messages and over twenty text messages from Tyreik. He'd blown her shit up. Chyna couldn't help but sit in the passenger seat and laugh. *Now this nigga wanna talk to me,* she smirked as her cell phone rang in her hand.

For a second she contemplated not answering his call but quickly changed her mind. She wanted to hear the desperation in his voice. Chyna fed off that shit. She never stayed out this late. She was sure Tyreik was losing his mind.

"What's up?" She answered dryly.

"Why the fuck you ain't been answering yo' phone?" He fumed.

"My phone died," she lied.

"Stop lyin'! Yo' fuckin' phone ain't die. You turned that muthafucka off."

"Ok, if I did? What you want, Tyreik, 'cause I ain't in the mood to argue wit' you."

"What I want?" He repeated appalled by her choice of words.

"Did I stutter? Yeah, what you want? You ain't have shit to say to me when we was at The Delmar so don't have shit to say to me now!"

"Fuck all that. Where you at, man?" He ignored her sarcasm.

"Out," Chyna screwed up her face.

"Out where?"

"None of yo' business!"

"Chyna, stop with the dumb shit. I'm at yo' crib and I'm tired as fuck. I'm ready to go to bed. When you coming home?" He groaned.

"I ain't got nothing to do wit' that. Where my daughter? Is she sleep?"

"Yeah, she was sleep when I got here. Now when you coming home? My dick hard. I'm tryin' to fuck."

"You betta grab the lotion and rub one out 'cause I ain't coming home." She stifled a laugh before ending the call.

Chyna sat grinning from ear to ear. Tyreik tried calling her back but was forwarded to voicemail. He was pissed to say the least.

"YOU THINK THE DEVIL IS JUST GOING TO LET YOU WALK OUT OF HELL WITHOUT A FIGHT? BAD MEN WANT LOVE TOO. IT'S YOUR JOB AS A WOMAN NOT TO CONFUSE DESIRE WITH WHAT YOU DESERVE. IT'S NOT A QUESTION OF WHETHER OR NOT HE LOVES YOU, IT'S HOW MUCH BULLSHIT THAT COMES WITH THE 'I LOVE YOU.' HOW MUCH BULLSHIT YOU'RE GOING TO PUT UP WITH.

REMEMBER, HE CAN BE SORRY FROM ANYWHERE. IT'S YOUR CHOICE OF WHETHER IT'S IN YOUR BED, OR THE CURB." – MEANDMRWRONG.COM

CHAPTER 28

That night, Chyna slept at Brooke's house. She didn't return home until later on that day. She expected to be met with the sound of yelling as soon as she walked through the door but instead was greeted with a hug from India.

"Mom!" India hugged her mother tight. "Where you been?"

"I spent the night at Auntie's house." Chyna squeezed India tight and kissed her forehead. "You ate yet?"

"Yeah, Tyreik bought me some Taco Bell for lunch."

"You clean up that room like I told you to?" Chyna arched her brow.

"Yes, Mom," India groaned rolling her eyes.

"Ok, good. Well let me go get my life in order and then me and you will do something fun together, ok?"

"Ok," India smiled gleefully.

Chyna slowly made her way up the steps. A huge knot was in the pit of her stomach. She was sure that she and Tyreik were about to have a showdown. When she hit her bedroom she expected to be met with a barrage of questions. Instead, she was greeted with a piercing silence. The bedroom was completely empty. Tyreik was nowhere to be found.

The only trace of him ever being there was the lingering smell of his cologne in the air, the unmade bed and a gigantic scuff mark on the wall. Chyna examined the mark closer. She quickly came to the conclusion that Tyreik had thrown his phone at the wall in a fit of rage.

"He really needs to grow up." She shook her head and threw down her bag and phone.

Irritated by his childish behavior and the fact that he left the bed looking a mess, Chyna threw the covers back. She couldn't function if her bed was unmade. To her surprise, as she straightened the sheets, she found Tyreik's cell phone. Stunned that he would've been careless enough to leave it behind, she slowly picked it up.

Merely touching his phone was an unwritten rule that she was breaking. She hardly ever went near the thing in fear of Tyreik's wrath. He would bite her head off if he walked in and caught her holding it. Chyna stared at the phone. Cupping it in the palm of her hand was like winning the gold medal at the Olympics. There was no way she could resist not going through it.

She might not get another chance. Now was the perfect time. It was just her luck that his phone wasn't locked. Tyreik must've taken the lock off since she didn't come home. Chyna didn't hesitate to go into his text messages first. In it she found nothing but text from her, his pot'nahs and business associates. If he did have a chick texting him, he'd already gotten rid of the evidence.

Next, she went through his pictures. There was hardly anything there except a few naked pics of her and screenshots of sneakers he wanted. The last thing she checked was his contacts. There were a few numbers saved under initials or single letters which she found odd. She automatically assumed they were chicks he fucked with numbers.

Chyna could feel her blood pressure rise as she scrolled through the numbers. Then her heart all but stopped beating when she came across Rema's name.

Tyreik swore that the thing between him and Rema were over. Why was her number in his phone again?

Chyna's palms began to sweat as a million thoughts swarmed her mind. What if they had started back fuckin' around? Had he been seeing her this whole time? Chyna couldn't bare the thought of going through the pain of him cheating on her again.

Before she could gather her thoughts, the familiar sound of Tyreik taking the steps two at a time pierced her ears. He must've realized he'd left his phone and came rushing back home. Chyna turned her head towards the stairs with tears in her eyes. She didn't even try to pretend like she wasn't going through his phone.

No, she was going to confront his lying, cheating-ass. Chyna stood looking like a wounded deer as Tyreik made it to the top of the steps. He eyed her with a stern expression on his face. He was still pissed that she hadn't come home the night before. He became even angrier when he spotted his phone in her hand.

"What you doing wit' my phone?"

"What it look like I was doing? I was going through it." Chyna quickly wiped her tears and regained her strength.

She refused to look weak in front of Tyreik. He'd broken her down one too many times.

"What I tell you about touching my shit?" He charged towards her and snatched his phone out of her hand. "This ain't yo' phone! You don't pay the bill on this muthafucka so don't touch it!" He pointed it in her face.

"I don't give a fuck about none of that! As long as you in this muthafucka I'ma touch whatever the fuck I want!"

"There you go threatening somebody 'cause yo' name on the lease. Get the fuck outta here wit' that! I got my own place, remember?"

"Mom! Can y'all stop fighting? I can hear y'all all the way downstairs!" India asked from the bottom of the staircase.

"India, go sit down!" Chyna yelled, feeling herself unraveling.

She knew she shouldn't have been arguing around her daughter but somehow it had become the norm for them. India rolled her eyes and did as she was told. She was so tired of her mother promising that things between her and Tyreik would get better. They would be at peace with one another only to be back at each others' throats days later. Their dysfunctional relationship was starting to wear on India. She only tolerated Tyreik for her mother's sake. She didn't hate him because at times he could be nice but most of the time he was an asshole.

"I'm finna go." Tyreik turned to leave.

"You ain't going nowhere!" Chyna pulled him back towards her. "Why the fuck you got that bitch number in yo' phone?" She gripped his arm tight.

"What bitch?" Tyreik eyed her confused.

"Don't play stupid. The bitch you cheated on me with."

"I ain't even tryin' to be funny but which bitch are you talkin' about?" Tyreik chuckled.

Chyna felt her heart sink. This nigga didn't give a fuck how he treated her. But how could she get mad at him? She'd allowed him to treat her like shit for years.

"Oh, so you think that shit is funny? I'm not laughing, Tyreik." She pushed his arm away.

"Yo, you buggin'. I ain't got time for this shit. You gon' make me late for my haircut." He tried to leave once more only for Chyna to jump in his path.

"Fuck yo' haircut. What you tryin' to get fly for Rema or that wavy hair bitch? You tryin' to look cute to impress they bummy-ass? I saw her name in your phone, Tyreik. Why after over ten years is this bitch name still poppin' up? You still fuckin' her, aren't you?" Chyna questioned feeling herself become sick.

"You're fuckin' insane." Tyriek eyed her in disbelief. "First you snap on me at the bar, then you don't come home, then you go through my phone on some ole Inspector Gadget shit and now you accuse me of cheating just 'cause you saw a bitch number in my phone? You're fuckin' crazy."

"If I'm crazy it's because you made me this way. I'm tired of dealing wit' you and yo' shit! Every other second it's something different wit' you. I can't ever get a moment to breathe without the rug being pulled from underneath me!"

"Ain't nobody cheating on you!" Tyreik barked.

"Then why is her number in your phone? You still haven't answered the question." Chyna cocked her head to the side.

"And I'm not 'cause I ain't did nothin'. Did you go through my call log? Do you see me calling her? Do you see her callin' me? Do you see us textin' each other? No! 'Cause ain't shit going on. Just the bullshit you conjuring up in yo' head!" He pointed his finger in her face like a gun.

"I'm tired of you accusing me of shit I ain't do. Now I'm done talkin'. I'm about to go get my haircut." He pushed her out the way and jogged down the steps.

"Uh ah, Tyreik! Come back! I'm not done talkin' to you!" Chyna raced behind him.

She would be damned if he thought he was getting away that easy. He had some serious explaining to do. The answers he'd given her just weren't good enough.

"Tyreik, I'm not playin' wit you!" She yelled.

"Do it look like I'm laughing?" He said over his shoulder as he continued to walk. "You wanna be on that bullshit, be on it by yo'self. You're not about to ruin my day."

"Ruin your day?" Chyna repeated barely able to breathe.

Tyreik loved switching things around and making Chyna feel like she was the problem.

"Nigga, how about you ruined my life!" Chyna mushed him in the back of his head as he made it to the front door.

"Mom, stop!" India pleaded jumping in front of her mother so she wouldn't hit Tyreik again. "Just let him go!"

Sorrow filled India's eyes. Her mom deserved so much more. She just didn't understand why she couldn't see it for herself. Tyreik spun around and charged towards her furiously.

"If I ruined your life then why the fuck you still wit' me? Huh? If I'm such a horrible-ass person, then why you keep coming back? 'Cause your full of shit, Chyna!" He mushed her in the forehead causing her head to jerk back. "You think life is one of them books you be writing. This ain't make-believe. This is real life and if you put yo' hands on me again I'ma fuck you up!"

"Nigga, do you think that if I could write the perfect man for me that it would be you?" Chyna's bottom lip quivered. "You out yo' muthafuckin' mind! I'ma tell you what's real life! What's real life is you fuckin' that bitch! And when I find proof of it I'ma be done fuckin' wit' your ass for good!" Chyna leaped across India and popped Tyreik in the face.

"Don't put yo' hands on me no more, man!" Tyreik reached over India and grabbed Chyna by the arm.

His grip was so tight that she felt like she was losing the blood circulation in her arm.

"Tyreik, stop! Let her go!" India begged trying to push him off her mother.

"That's yo' ignorant-ass mama! Tell her to keep her fuckin' hands off of me! I told her to gon'!" He threw her arm down angrily.

"Explain to me how you mad! I'm the one that caught you on some bullshit." Chyna tried to step past India to no avail.

Not wanting things to escalate any further, Tyreik opened the front door and slammed it shut behind him, almost causing the glass to shatter.

"Don't be slamming my goddamn door!" Chyna fumed. "Move, India!" She tried to push her out the way.

"Mom, chill. Just let him leave." India cornered her mother.

Chyna knew she should listen to her daughter. She was right but the rage inside of her veins had taken over. She couldn't see anything but red. She had to make him hurt. Tyreik had disrespected her for the last time. Not hearing her daughter, Chyna pushed her out of the way and raced out of the door. To her dismay, Tyreik had already made it to his car.

That didn't stop her from standing in front of his truck and slamming her fist into the hood. She didn't care that it was broad daylight or that her neighbors were outside. She needed him to see how much pain she was in. Tyreik however didn't care about her feelings. All he cared about was getting away from her stupid-ass before something crazy popped off.

He was so mad he was liable to slap the shit outta Chyna. The last thing he needed was the cops being called. Without paying attention to his surroundings, he placed the car in reverse and rammed his foot on the gas. The truck went flying backwards into the street. What Tyreik failed to realize was that a school bus was coming towards him.

Chyna's eyes widened with fear as the school bus crashed into the side of Tyreik's truck. The impact was so hard that the truck flipped over three times and landed on the roof. A blood curdling scream escaped from Chyna's lungs as she ran towards the driver's side. There Tyreik was dangling upside down with blood trickling from his forehead, nose and mouth. Broken glass was everywhere.

"India, call 911!" Chyna screamed trying to unlock the door but the door was stuck.

India ran back in the house and did as she was told.

"Baby! Are you ok?" Chyna sobbed feeling like she was dying.

Tyreik couldn't even find the strength to respond. His heart rate was declining by the second. All he could do was take short, shallow breaths.

"Baby, answer me. Tell me you're ok. You have to be ok, Tyreik. I'm sorry. I'm so sorry." She wept caressing the side of his face.

Then the unthinkable happened. Tyreik's eyes started to flutter. It was taking every fiber of his being to keep his eyes open.

"No-no-no-no-no-no! You have to stay awake. Don't you fall asleep, Tyreik!" Chyna sobbed trying to keep him focused.

But Tyreik couldn't hold on any longer. His eyes were too heavy. With the little strength he had, he took one last look at Chyna then allowed his eyes to close.

"Noooooooo! Tyreik, wake up!" She patted his face repeatedly. "Wake up, please. Tyreik! I'm sorry! Wake up! Tyreik! WAAAAAAAAAAKE UP!!!!!!"

CPSIA information can be obtained at www.ICGtesting.com
Printed in the USA
LVOW10s0426280516

490349LV00017B/1029/P